LINGERGING IN THE DARK

ANDREW LAMONT

Dedicated to the loving memory of Shaun Beattie, the brightest of souls (1997-2019)

LINGERING IN THE DARK

Chapter One

Franklin and Sarah Oswald's new lives were beginning. No more relying on others for things they needed. They were married; they had bought their own house, ominous though it might have been. Although they had never seen it in person – only in photographs – it had an indescribably unsettling feeling about it. In spite of this, neither of them could escape an irresistible pull the place had over them.

The sun had shone brightly since daybreak. As time went on, however, clouds moved in. Now, the clouds darkened overhead as they grew closer to their new home. Though neither of them spoke of it, Sarah and Franklin thought it was rather strange: rain had not been forecast. Neither of them cared, though; they were starting their new life. This time, they had promised each other, things would be better.

Finally, after driving for several hours, they reached the last village before they would arrive at the town, they would call home. A quaint little seaside village; the townsfolk smiled and waved as they drove on. Ordinarily used to not acknowledging people, the pair were surprised to find themselves waving back.

Everyone they saw wore high-end clothes. The ladies walked by in exquisite dresses; arms locked with men in sharp Armani suits.

As they drove by, Franklin stared at the buildings, unable to suppress his interest. The buildings towered above the car, looming, blocking out the sunlight. The townsfolk marched around, acknowledging one another with quick smiles.

Given that neither of them had eaten since early that morning, and it was now almost evening, Sarah and Franklin were relieved to pull into a small restaurant fifty miles from their new home.

This restaurant, uninspiringly named The Restaurant, was made of red brick which had browned with age. It was far from the most welcoming place they had visited. But, rather like the house, there was something irresistible about it.

They barely gave consideration to the empty parking lot. They were just relieved the complete lack of cars allowed them to park right next to the entrance.

As soon as Franklin opened the driver's-side door, the dropping temperature became unignorable. Sarah, who rarely felt the chill, even commented on the cold.

As they entered the building, a wall of heat hit them.

Discoloured beige carpets stretched as far as they could see, and did not match the dark wooden pillars, or the walls with black-and-white photographs of the village upon them. People bustled around carrying food and drink, their faces lacking any expression.

As they stood waiting to be served, Franklin and Sarah looked around. The diners didn't exactly look as though they were filled with joy at the prospect of eating there. Other than the shuffling sound of footsteps, the place was eerily silent.

"Can I help you?" came a cold, almost lifeless voice from behind them. Before they had a chance to turn around, the person moved to stand in front of them. His face was paler than death, stern and hard-lined.

"We would like a table for two, please," Franklin replied with a half-smile, hoping that his effort would liven the man up a little. It did not. The man's face hardened further.

In response, the waiter whipped out two menus from the desk, then turned and walked away. Assuming they were supposed to follow, Franklin and Sarah took each other's hand and walked briskly to catch up with him.

It was an inescapable fact that the diners were all watching them with unblinking eyes. The couple, although slightly uneasy, were too captivated by the lifeless waiter to ask why the people were staring without any attempt at hiding it. Truth be told, they didn't care. They refused to allow negativity to taint their new beginning.

Though they were somewhat unsettled by the people in The Restaurant, they tried not to let it bother them: they would only be in there for an hour or so, and they didn't have to discuss the matter to each know they would never be back. It was true: never would they return. But the reason was not what they thought.

The waiter thumped the menus down onto a table, then flicked a switch to put on a dim light which barely illuminated the lampshade, never mind the menus. With that, he stalked away without saying another word.

Franklin pulled a seat out for Sarah before taking his own. He flicked through the menu, thoroughly unimpressed with the choices and their vague descriptions.

Soup.

"What do you reckon the soup is, Sarah?" he asked.

Without any warning, and without making any sound upon his approach, the waiter answered, "The soup is chicken soup. The meat is beef. What do you want to drink?"

After regaining control of their heart rates, Sarah and Franklin ordered tap water. The waiter stalked away again, muttering something under his breath.

Sarah found it odd that there were no windows other than the glass panel in the door. She hadn't noticed until that moment just how dark The Restaurant was, just how unkind these people were. Maybe I am being slightly harsh, she thought to herself, although she wasn't certain that was true. Something about this place unnerved her.

Sarah had never been one to be judgemental of people. She always looked for the best in everyone. Her belief was this: if you are at the very least pleasant to those around you, they will be pleasant in return. Now, though, she was beginning to question that belief. Perhaps the waiter is having a bad day, she considered.

Within a few minutes, the waiter returned with the water, thrusting it onto the table with such vigour that Franklin was surprised it didn't spill. Not even a drop fell out of the glasses.

"Thank you so much," Sarah said, smiling. "We've had a long drive, and I'm parched. I'm Sarah, by the way. What's your name?" She held out her hand, presuming he would take it.

"I am Derek," he replied before turning and walking away without smiling.

Franklin knew Sarah was an expert at hiding being upset – mostly because she didn't want to cause anyone else to be unhappy, but also because she refused to let anyone worry about her. Too many people had worried, too many people had been hurt … everything changed when it happened.

He reached over, took his wife's hand, and smiled gently. Neither spoke, but they both knew what the other thought: let's just get through this meal and leave. Quickly.

When Derek shuffled back to take their food order, he did not say one word. Franklin and Sarah asked for the beef, and Derek slithered away once again.

Franklin excused himself to go to the bathroom. As he was walking around trying to find it, he could not help but notice how intensely the people were looking at him. Not wanting to show his discomfort, he sped up.

Why was everybody staring at them? What, he wondered, was so interesting about them? These people didn't even know them.

Searching earnestly for the bathroom, he saw that more people were watching him. Everywhere he turned, it seemed, there were five more people glaring at him, their vicious eyes burrowing into his body.

Eventually, he found the sign pointing to the bathroom. Letting out a sigh of relief, Franklin walked down the stairs. Every step groaned as though in pain. He knew he was letting his overactive imagination get the better of him, but the noises almost sounded like a frightened child crying. He put his hand on the banister to prevent himself from falling through the stairs, which he thought was a very real possibility given the obvious age of the building.

Reaching the bottom of the stairs, he opened a coal-black door and found himself in the bathroom. The aggressively bright light blinded him, and he had to squint to grow accustomed to it. There was one corner, though, in the far left, where the light didn't reach. He wasn't sure why, but something within him told him to avoid that corner. At all costs.

A man stalked out of the shadows as Franklin was washing his hands. His skin clung to his bones like a new-born baby to its mother. His eyes were sunken and were surrounded by purple circles. His ragged clothes hung off his body. Franklin didn't know what to do – how to help the man, or even if he could help. Nevertheless, he knew he had to at least try.

Franklin decided the man was in his thirties, or thereabouts, despite at a glance resembling someone in his nineties.

"Do not go there," the man screeched. "Do not go there. Whatever you do."

Franklin's brow furrowed in confusion. What was he talking about?

When asked, the man simply repeated himself, his eyes widening with every word. He shook and repeatedly yelled, "Do not go there! You hear me? Do not go there."

"I don't know what you mean," Franklin replied, and made towards the door.

Despite his condition, the skeletal man moved with the speed of a startled spider. He slammed the door shut and grabbed Franklin's hands. Tears streamed down his face. "Please," he begged. "Do not go there."

Franklin, unsure what else to do, assured him he wouldn't – even though he wasn't sure where there was.

Tearfully, the man thanked him, grabbing his hands again and again as tears soaked his face.

"When did you last eat?" Franklin asked in concern.

The poor man simply shrugged.

Smiling with melancholy, Franklin said, "Come upstairs. My wife and I will get you a meal."

The man could only nod in response.

As they made their way up the stairs, the man continually thanked Franklin for agreeing not to go there. Franklin nodded and smiled.

When they approached their table, Franklin saw the beef was already served on two plates. Sarah, who had been waiting for Franklin to come back, looked up to see the skeletal man standing next to her husband, who had pulled over an additional chair. The man dropped into the chair like a discarded bag of trash.

Sarah fought to keep control of her rising emotions. "We're going to order you some food," she said instantly, without even asking what the man's circumstances were. She knew that, in most scenarios, it was better to help those in need than to make them explain themselves. She got to her feet and went to find the waiter.

She approached the counter where an equally unkind-looking woman with grey hair tied into a tight bun stood, glaring at her with something resembling hatred.

"Could we please have another plate of beef?" she asked, trying to smile.

"I am hardly going to say no. That's ten pounds," the woman replied, before screaming the order into the kitchen and then taking out a pack of chewing gum and chucking a piece into her mouth.

Sarah stared at the woman, perturbed.

"Is there something else I can help you with?" the woman asked apathetically.

"No, that's all, thanks," Sarah said, handing over the money, forcing a smile onto her face.

"Then go back to your table and stop bothering me."

The words hurt Sarah more than they would anybody else. People often called her over-sensitive when she was growing up, which hurt her even more. She could feel tears forming in her eyes as she walked back to the table.

The man was rocking back and forth in his seat. Sarah assured him his food would be there soon. He responded with a curt nod.

Franklin and Sarah, not wanting to wait for their food to go cold, started to eat. As they did so, the skeletal man snapped, "My name is Gordon. You are Franklin and Sarah Oswald, and you must not go there."

Sarah's eyes shot to Franklin, who mouthed the question: "Did you tell him our names?"

Franklin shook his head once.

Immediately, fear seeped into every corner of Sarah's body, every fibre of her being controlled by the terrible emotion. They ate the rest of their meal in silence. Just as they finished, Derek brought Gordon's food and slammed the plate onto the table before moving away. Strange, Franklin thought, he looks like he's floating.

"Well," Sarah began, gesturing for Franklin to collect his things, "we should probably be going. Long drive ahead. I hope you enjoy your meal."

They got to their feet and hurried to the door. As they were about to pull it open, a small child came running over to them, her face drained of all colour. Her eyes, which were bluer than the ocean, coupled with her pale expression, gave her face an oddly porcelain appearance. The young girl shouted after them, pleading with them to go back home. No tears flowed down her cheeks. Instead, her unblinking gaze burrowed into them, through skin and bones.

The girl ran out of The Restaurant and grabbed Sarah by the arm, digging her nails into her flesh. "Don't go to that house," she yelled. "Whatever happens, do not go there. Go back home. Better to be out of pocket than dead."

Franklin, who had never been one to become violent, pushed the young girl to the ground. "Never take hold of my wife like that again," he roared, unsure where this aggression was coming from. "How do you know we've bought a house?"

The girl rolled her eyes. "You have never been seen here before, and there's only one reason new people come to this corner of the world: you have bought the house which must not be lived in. Bad things happen there."

Franklin, growing ever more indignant, told Sarah to get into the car. The couple, of course, had heard the stories from the real estate agent who sold them the house. Apparently, it was haunted. Sarah climbed into the vehicle, and switched on the radio: she had no intention of hearing the conversation outside. Stories like those unsettled her.

She didn't believe in ghosts or spirits. However, what she did believe was that fate can be tempted.

Having studied History, Franklin had always been fascinated by supposed ghost sightings, but he knew that they always came down to imagination. Never had he come across a story with substantial proof. Tales of macabre entities tended to involve unstable parents who thought they'd seen someone who had died years before.

Although he'd grown up being fascinated by the tales, Franklin hadn't ever quite understood why people had such confidence in them. Moreover, he had no idea why parents insisted on passing the tales onto their children.

Had Sarah and he had the baby, they would have raised it lovingly, telling it fairy tales and fables. However, they wouldn't have let it believe it had seen a ghost. Those fiendish tales disturbed children: he would not have been one of those parents, had they had the child. He would never have deliberately frightened it.

Neither of them put much stock into the stories of the tragedies from the house. After all, it had been going cheap, below even their budget. Knowing how dreadful the market could be, they had purchased it immediately.

"Go back to your parents," Franklin instructed the girl, "and in future, don't bother strangers." With that, he climbed into the car, put the key in the ignition, turned it, and drove away at speed. As they exited the car park, he and

Sarah vowed to each other never to return to that place. The people, they agreed, were too bound by superstitious nonsense. Sarah felt some modicum sympathy for them: it must be horrendous to live in fear all the time; to believe that a house over fifty miles away, was haunted and that it could somehow affect them. Not that she let Franklin know.

She looked through the windshield and up at the sky. "Those clouds," she murmured, "are darker than ever."

Chapter Two

Thirty minutes later, Franklin and Sarah once again found themselves in the middle of nowhere, driving along narrow, winding roads. They had been listening to the radio, but lost signal three miles back. The first time in England they had lost signal. Now, completely cut off from the rest of the world, even their sat nav had cut out. Luckily, they knew that they just had to follow the road.

Sarah hadn't spoken since they had got back into the car, for which Franklin was grateful. He was struggling to avoid potholes.

The sky grew more ominous with every passing mile. Fog obscured their view of the road ahead. Before long, the mist had become so dense that they had to slow for their own safety.

"Can you see much?" Sarah asked, as Franklin slowed down even further. He shook his head and pressed harder on the brake. "Maybe you should slow down a little bit," she suggested. "We don't know when a tight turn could appear. If we go off the road, we're in trouble."

"You're right," Franklin responded, and did so. Sarah turned and looked at him, looking as though she had something to ask, but wasn't quite sure how to do so. "What is it?"

"I'd just like to know how long it's going to be until I can read your book," Sarah said, half-joking.

For as long as he could remember, Franklin had wanted to be a writer. At first, he had assumed he would pen non-fiction books, but in his teens, he had found a new appreciation for fiction. In particular, he enjoyed murder mysteries. He had sped through all the classics, and all the other ones he could find. He had decided to start writing his own novel a year ago but had rarely spoken about it in public. As a matter of fact, Sarah believed she was the only person Franklin had told.

They spoke a little about the plot of the book, Sarah listening with great interest. He had told her everything about the novel apart from the identity of the murderer.

Soon the fog began to lift, so Franklin sped up slightly and they continued on their way.

As they drove along the narrow road, not going above thirty miles an hour, the radio caught onto a channel they hadn't heard of before. Neither of them recognised the origins of the hosts' thick accents, and the morbid subject matter of the conversation told them it was a local channel. Surely, no national stations would air these things. Franklin, irritated at himself for being so interested, turned the volume up slightly.

"They didn't think to leave when these things started happening?" someone on the radio questioned. "They didn't even consider leaving?"

"No, they stayed because they refused to believe the signs they were being shown."

"And what happened in the end?" the person asked.

"They went missing the next week. Four days later, Barbara Locket was found in the lake nearby, and William Locket was found hanging from the tree."

"Let me guess," someone else chipped in, "the deaths were ruled as a suicide?"

"That's right. They always are. People try to explain away things they don't want to understand. Janet Baxter struck again."

Franklin and Sarah turned to look at one another, shock and confusion riddling their expressions. "Baxter," Sarah whispered, almost in disbelief.

"Don't worry yourself," Franklin answered. "They are dead; they can't do anything to us. These are just people's imaginations."

The Baxter family were the initial owners of the house they were moving into. Although he didn't know every detail, he knew the four of them had been murdered. For some reason, which he could not fathom, this had led people to believe the house was cursed.

Eerie instrumental music started to play, causing Sarah's hairs to stand on end. Franklin didn't for a second believe the tragic deaths were the works of macabre spirits, nor did he believe they had anything to do with the Baxter family, as the people on the radio were clearly alluding to.

"Thank you for joining us on The Unexplained. Join us tomorrow at the same time, when we will be talking about the hauntings of Ethel Green. Until then, folks, stay vigilant."

Sarah squirmed in her seat before turning to look at her husband. Her eyes were wide and teary. Franklin didn't dare engage her in conversation at that moment. Sarah was incredibly easy to scare. The slightest unexpected noise at night would keep her up for hours. He started flicking through other stations, trying to find something – anything – else to listen to. He was unsuccessful, and ended up switching the machine off.

"Better to ignore than to entertain fools," his father used to say. Just the thought of that man-made saying had Franklin sit up straight and keep quiet. Although he knew, or rather thought, his father had loved him, he was unsure of how genuine it had been. He had never met someone so severe and so perennially serious since his father died.

Franklin missed him, yes. But, more than that, he missed the father he wished he had had. He had grown up with one sister, Anna, and one brother, Luke. Nowadays he only spoke with his sister as Luke had grown more objectionable as he matured and had decided to cut ties with them all over a Christmas argument.

Thinking about it, it seemed painfully ridiculous that things had gotten so out of hand. Despite being invited, Luke hadn't attended Franklin's and Sarah's wedding.

Sarah, seeing Franklin's change in demeanour, and knowing the usual causes of his sudden mood swings, said gently, "He can't hurt you, Frank. You're safe with me. He can never harm you again."

Franklin didn't answer, too busy concentrating on the road ahead. He knew Sarah had spoken, but didn't quite catch what she had said: the sound of a leather belt connecting with skin was too loud in his mind.

The car accelerated gradually. They were getting further and further from their past. But, at the same time, they were getting closer and closer to the house. Closer. Closer. Closer.

Angry, charcoal-grey clouds threatened to burst above them as they approached a sign welcoming them to another town: Mortville.

"I think there might be a thunderstorm," Sarah said, hoping to pull her husband away from his thoughts, at least for a while. One of the reasons they considered themselves so perfect for each other was because they were able to keep each other safe.

"I— I think you're right," he replied, the words barely more than a whisper.

"Where are the keys?" Sarah asked.

"According to the person I signed the cheque for, they are under the yellow flowerpot, just behind the pillar." He paused for a moment. "I assume it'll be easy to find."

"I'm sure it will be," Sarah replied with a forced smile. "Would you like to put the radio back on?"

"There's not much point. We're less than ten minutes away," Franklin answered. "Unless that was a hint?"

"No hint."

For the next couple minutes, they sat in silence, looking around at the town. At first it struck them as odd that they saw no people wandering around, but when they looked up at the dark clouds, they understood. There was no getting away from it: they were in for a storm.

The town seemed idyllic: it even had a square with a fountain in its centre; a lake at the bottom of the hill the car was currently climbing; a somewhat long road with a great number of small shops: a butcher; a greengrocer, and so on. At the end of the road, a cathedral towered over every other building.

Quaint little cafes lined the streets, all of which had canopies and little white tables and chairs outside. The only thing Franklin and Sarah didn't see was a school, which they thought was unusual. They had assumed there would be one, but perhaps everybody in the town schooled their own children.

Without warning, Franklin stopped the car.

"What are you doing?" Sarah enquired, her brows furrowed.

"Look," he replied, pointing upwards. "It's our new home."

"How many floors are there?" she asked.

Franklin thought for a moment. "Three, if you include the loft."

Looming above them, shrouded in shadow, lingering under the dark clouds, was their house. Blacker-than-soot bricks gave it a sense of ostentatious gloom. A ragged and decaying fence ran around the grounds, and looked as though it hadn't been touched in decades. A single grey tree stood in front of the house; a noose hung from its largest branch. Franklin and Sarah averted their eyes.

They drove on.

As they were pulling into the grounds, Sarah looked up at the windows and couldn't help but screw her face. The panes of glass were grotesquely filthy. She couldn't see through them. It was as if the windows had been painted over, and left to rot along with the rest of the estate.

Sarah opened the car door and got out, while Franklin went to find the yellow flowerpot. She wandered around the outside of the house, trying to find a window she could actually see through. Her efforts were in vain.

"Frank," she yelled.   "Please   tell   me this house has electricity."

Franklin smiled. "I assume so."

Sarah couldn't describe the relief filling her heart at his answer. She took a napkin she'd taken from The Restaurant out of her pocket and wiped a window with it. Her napkin came away blackened.

That's not what concerned her, though. What did concern her was the lily-white, spectral face staring at her through the glass. A scream built up within her, but refused to come out.

Trembling, she made to run into the arms of her husband – but she couldn't. It was as if some invisible force was keeping her from moving. Unwillingly, Sarah turned her head. Whoever, whatever, dwelled on the other side of that window watched her with wide eyes.

"You have to get out of here," the voice of a young boy said.

Sarah closed her eyes and tried to scream. When no sound came out, she fell to the ground and rocked back and forth. In the distance, a bird squawked. Or ... was it a child screaming?

Despite not being able to speak, Sarah tried to tell Franklin what had happened. When it became clear to her, he didn't understand, she took him by the hand and practically dragged him to where she had been standing.

She pointed through the dreary window, which had steamed up. Franklin, still not comprehending, raised an eyebrow. Irritated, Sarah wrote the following word into the window: Face.

Franklin understood what she was trying to convey to him but didn't believe her. "Your imagination is working against you, my love," he told her as kindly as he could. "It must have been that radio show we caught the end of. You have nothing to worry about: I'm here. More to the point, we're miles away from danger."

All at once, Sarah's voice returned to her, with a vengeance. She roared, "I didn't imagine it! A young boy was on the other side of this window. He looked terrified. We have to help him. There must be something we can do."

Her husband, taken aback by her outburst, gave in. "Okay, why don't we take the cases into the house, and then go and look around for this boy. If we find him, we'll do everything we can to help him. If we don't," he said, smiling, "we will carry on with our lives."

Sarah knew full well Franklin didn't believe her, but she nodded, and they walked back to the car. As they traversed the barren wasteland that was their new garden, she said, "After that, we need to clean this place. Repugnant doesn't even come close."

"Yes," Franklin said. "We do."

He opened the boot of the car and they removed their suitcases one by one and took them into the house. When all the suitcases were inside, Franklin closed the boot of the car, locked the vehicle and entered their new house.

As soon as he had closed the door behind him, an almighty crash came from the sky. The clouds opened and the rain came down in torrents. The water bounced off the car and the ground, and hammered on the roof like hailstones, to the degree that Franklin and Sarah worried that it might cave in. However, that was not what the couple should have been worrying about. Far worse fates awaited them, and they didn't even know it. Perhaps, if they had, the story would have been different.

"Welcome to our new home," Sarah said, smiling weakly. "Let's go and find the boy and help him. This place is freezing. He must be so frightened."

Chapter Three

Sarah searched the downstairs of the house, fighting to ignore the many layers of dust through which she moved. That poor boy, she thought. He must be so frightened.

Never before had she been in such a disgusting place, and never before had she felt so uneasy. Although the precise cause of her unease eluded her, she couldn't shake the feeling, no matter how hard she tried. It was as though something was watching her from the shadows … something which wished her ill.

"Little boy," she called out, repeating her cry several times a minute. "We're not going to hurt you. Come out, and let us help you."

When no boy came forward, Sarah shook her head in dismay. Why wouldn't he come forward? The little boy, surely …

Had she seen anything, though? Maybe I did imagine him, she thought. After all, it is a new place. I know the stories.

Sarah felt utterly repulsed by the dust coating every surface. She glanced around the place, at the furniture, at the portraits on the walls, at the mantlepieces, at the carpets.

Everything in the house reminded Sarah of her grandmother. From the furniture, to the wallpaper, to the carpets, nothing looked new. Her grandmother had enjoyed living in the early nineteenth century even when Sarah had been born.

She called to her husband, asking him to bring in the cleaning things they'd packed after being told of the townspeople's refusal to go anywhere near the house.

Franklin picked up a cleaning spray and a cloth, and started cleaning the windows. Sarah turned her attention to the mantles.

"When was this place last cleaned, do you think?" she said.

"If it's all the same to you, my love, I'd rather not think about it."

They both laughed, and continued cleaning. They dusted, and hoovered, and mopped in the kitchen.

Sarah asked, "Aren't you glad we brought food with us, and don't need to go shopping today?"

Franklin nodded. "More than words could ever convey."

Thirty minutes passed before Sarah had finished dusting the surfaces. Apart from the dust, everything was clean. Too tired to think anything of it, Sarah put the duster into a cupboard, and headed upstairs.

They walked upstairs. Sarah was almost certain she heard a child singing a version of

Mary Had A Little Lamb, but when she got to the first landing and saw the violent swaying of the trees, she put it down to the wind. Once she had heard it, she couldn't block it out. It wailed as though in pain.

His voice was all but drowned out by the abrupt howling of the wind.

Neither Sarah nor Franklin could stifle yawns while they unpacked essentials: clothes, toiletries, food.

They looked around at the bedroom. Although it did strike them as strange that the upstairs was immaculate, they were more relieved than concerned. Sarah said, "I'm going to look in the loft." When Franklin looked at her quizzically, she continued, "I need to make sure the boy I saw isn't up there. Could you please put the bedclothes on?"

"For sure," Franklin replied with a smile. Sarah strolled to the door which led to the loft, then shivered. We need to work out the heating, she thought. The forecast for the area was a sea wind coming in the next day. The cold would be merciless.

A spiralling, uneven, stone staircase led up to the loft. Better be careful. It would be easy to fall here.

She continued up the steps, getting colder with every stride. A door stood ajar at the top of the staircase. Sarah stopped dead, that same ungodly force keeping her in place. Though she tried, she couldn't move; she couldn't even blink.

It was inexplicable: her hairs stood on end as a chill swept over her. Her heartrate quickened. If she hadn't known better, she might have believed there was something trying to stop her from going into that loft. If only she had turned back …

Abruptly, whatever force had been holding her released her.

An earth-shaking creak sounded as Sarah pushed the door open. A blast of Baltic air slammed into her as she stepped over the threshold. Entering the loft was a strange experience: Sarah felt as though there were people watching her. "Little boy?" she whimpered. "I know you are scared. You needn't fear us." Unfortunately, Sarah was the one who should have been afraid. A lesson she would only learn when it was too late.

The loft was stacked full of junk and seemed to contain a mountain range of dust. Freezing wind blew without restraint, wailing as though in pain – or in warning? You're working against yourself, Sarah told herself.

Despite the fact she continued to repeat those sentences in her mind, she couldn't ignore the resemblance of the wailing wind to words: Get out.

Behind her, floorboards creaked. She stiffened, her heart thrashing, her chest heaving up and down like waves upon a violent sea. Refusing to turn around, she simply stood there, trying not to scream. Just your imagination, she told herself again and again.

The wind grew ever more vicious, hammering against the house like the furies of Ancient Greece.

Battling every fibre, every instinct, of her being that told her to run, Sarah remained motionless. Her hairs stood on end, sharp as blades. Floorboards creaked, becoming louder with every passing second. Sarah remembered she was not alone ... Franklin was downstairs; he'd be the one making those noises from downstairs. Right?

Wrong.

Whatever was causing that sound, it was right behind her, moving closer.

A breath on her neck, a brush against her skin. Sarah longed to scream, but didn't dare. Though she was desperate to run, she couldn't.

An indescribable stench attacked her senses. Behind her, something screamed. At once, she laughed despite her exhaustion and frustration: over in the corner of the loft, a window was open. From where she was standing, it looked as though it had been hooked on the latch.

Briskly, Sarah strode across the room to close the window. Although she had, in her own opinion, created the entire scenario in her mind, she wanted out. She wanted to be with Franklin. She wanted her old life back.

"No," she snapped at herself. "Stop it."

After closing the window, she made a bee-line for the door, and bulleted down the stairs, the crashing of her footsteps resounding in her ears.

Before going into the bedroom, she went to the bathroom to regain control of her breathing. Truth be told, because she loved and trusted Franklin with everything she had, she didn't want him to know how unutterably terrified she was. He would only worry.

She put on the light, and at once decided to get new light bulbs, ones that produced less aggressive glare. The bright white walls temporarily blinded her.

Once the tap was running, she let heavy breaths pour out of her body. Sitting down on the side of the bathtub, she counted to ten slowly and named five things she could see, touch and hear. Grounding herself was becoming a little easier with each passing day. For that, at least, she was grateful.

"Keep yourself calm," she whispered. "You can't lose yourself. Not again."

She heard a scream, followed by a screech. All at once she was back there, cloaked in blood, surrounded by flashing lights and wailing sirens. Then silence.

Turning off the tap, she left and headed through the house. Franklin smiled as she hurried into the bedroom. "You look as ready for bed as I am," he told her, opening his arms. His embrace was her safe place.

"I love you," she whimpered.

In response, Franklin pulled her closer. "I love you, too. I always have and I always will. We're going to get through this, my darling."

Snuggled up to her husband, Sarah said quietly, "Thank you." She slipped under the covers. "Thank you for who you are, and what you do for me. I don't deserve a husband like you."

She didn't even have to look at him to know he was shaking his head. "If I believed that, I wouldn't have married you," he replied. "You are a wonderful person, Sarah. You deserve everything you want, and more." He wrapped another comforting arm around her.

She wanted to curl up into a ball beside him, wishing more than anything that she could be the person she thought he wanted. "I love you," she told him again, hoping he knew just how much. There were not enough words in the English language – no, in any language – to express the magnitude of her adoration.

"I love you, too. Get some sleep. You've had a long day. I'll see you in the morning, my love."

Sarah nodded, and Franklin turned off the light. Mere moments later, Franklin was dreaming of his wife. Sarah, however, couldn't sleep. She laid there, staring at the ceiling. It was fortunate, in that moment at least, that neither of them saw the bluish glow coming from outside their door, spilling under the gap.

After lingering in the dark for a few moments, the light vanished, leaving the house to dwell under the blackness of night.

***

As the night dragged on, the weather worsened. An almighty crash awoke Franklin, who lurched forward, taking a moment or two to realise where he was. He happened to glance out the window and, despite his drowsy state, he saw the rain thrashing through the moonlight.

"It's nothing, Sarah," he said. "The rain's heavy, that's all. I'm going to the bathroom, I'll be back in a minute."

Franklin could barely keep his eyes open as he made his way along the corridor. When he saw a young girl climbing up the staircase to the loft, he didn't spend even a second thinking about it. Believing he was still half-asleep, he continued on his way.

After flicking the switch and squinting to see in the sudden blast of light, Franklin turned on the tap so that the water would be warm when he needed it.

The sensation of hot water was welcome: the bathroom, he realised, was the only room in the house without a radiator. Frost was latched onto the window. The chill that night was merciless.

As he ran his hands through the water, Franklin heard footsteps outside the bathroom. Sarah must be getting up for a drink, he assumed.

"Would you like me to get you something?" he asked, but there was no response other than the footsteps increasing in volume and pace, indicating that the person was running down the hallway.

He furrowed his brow, and turned around. What is she doing?

If only he had looked outside, he would have seen it was indeed Sarah – but he would also have seen distant, cold lifelessness in her eyes. She was not herself in these moments. Some spirit had taken her by the hand, and was leading her down the stairs. If only he had looked. Maybe things would have ended differently. It's unlikely, but we'll never know.

Instead, he headed back to his bedroom and, as he hadn't turned on the light in either the hallway or the bedroom, he was blissfully unaware that his beloved wife was no longer in the bed. Franklin slept alone that night. Maybe it was for the best that he didn't know what was happening. Maybe not.

As sleep claimed him, the light of the moon subsided. Lingering in the dark, evil was coming out to play.

Chapter Four

Downstairs, wearing only a nightgown – gloriously unperturbed by the bitter cold or the thunderous storm outside – Sarah moved, quiet as a whisper, from room to room. Her hands shifted from object to object as she moved them from one place to another. Her eyes, though they were open, saw nothing.

Gracefully, she moved through the downstairs floor of the house. But then her direction changed. Now she was heading for the basement, the only room as yet unexplored by the couple.

She didn't blink once as she made her way through the darkened rooms. Under the influence of whatever had just taken her by the hand, she moved swiftly, oblivious to the unpierced darkness within the house.

She stood outside the door that led to the basement, her hand wrapped around the handle. A cool breeze shot through the ground floor – not that Sarah noticed. Turning her hand, she opened the door, and began her descent into the unknown. Although she stared with blank eyes, she moved as though she had lived in the house her entire life. She even anticipated the turn of that god-forsaken staircase.

When she reached the bottom, Sarah turned the corner she couldn't have previously known existed. Moving past the glaring eyes of the three orange spirits of the Baxter family, she glided to the centre of the floor.

In front of her, the spirit of a young boy sang. His voice was soft and calming. He, like the other spirits, wore nightclothes with a dark mark on the chest.

Now she knelt in the middle of the basement floor, moving back and forth, back and forth, back and forth. She swayed in her dirtied nightgown, moving to the beat of the spirit's song. As the boy sang, he smiled at Sarah, who unwillingly, unknowingly, responded with a smile of her own.

The four spirits formed a square around her, observing without acting, for now. When the youngest spirit, that of the nine-year-old boy, moved away from Sarah, she simply continued to kneel.

The mother spirit – formerly known as Missus Judith Baxter – stared at Sarah, her eyes unshifting. The father spirit – Charles Baxter – glared. Next was the spirit of an eleven-year-old girl – who had been Barbara Baxter – who watched, smiling at the woman's beauty and the way her hair flowed so elegantly down to her elbow. And the spirit of the young boy – Henry Baxter, who once had been so full of energy – simply looked at the woman he had watched dance and wished he could grow up and become a man. But he never would.

"What do you think, dear?" Charles enquired, bringing the silence to an end. Outside, the rain continued to hammer, its ferocity increasing with each drop. "What do we do? I don't think we need fear."

Janet Baxter's spirit turned from Sarah to her husband, then to her children and back to her husband. She smiled. "We do what we always do. We let ourselves indulge in trust before, and look what happened. No. We continue to do what we have been doing all these years. But we bide our time."

Barbara shook her head. "No, Mother. I agree with Father."

The mother looked somewhat irritated as she held out her hand to her daughter. "My child, it is, in that case, fortunate for us that you do not make the decisions. We do this out of love, out of our duty and privilege to protect you and your brother."

She turned to her son, who seemed uncertain where to turn or what action to take. Raising an eyebrow, the mother asked her son the question she had asked many, many times before: "What are you thinking, Henry?"

Before the young boy could answer, his mother gestured toward the door which led to the staircase. He understood. "You know what is best, Mother."

Obediently, Henry took Sarah by the hand, and led her back up the steps to the ground floor. He escorted her to the settee, where she lay down and closed her unseeing eyes. Slumber enveloped her.

With that, the spirits faded away to wait patiently for the right moment, the perfect time to attack. Soon, the mother decided. Soon we will strike.

***

As night became morning, the sun rose, shining its brilliant rays through the trees and into the sitting room of the house. Franklin, still enjoying his final good sleep, had not awoken or even stirred since going to the bathroom, in spite of the events occurring mere metres below him.

Sarah opened her eyes, awoken by the sunlight. Consciousness came slowly at first, then all at once. With a start, she lurched forward, her gaze darting from wall to wall, from ceiling to floor. But then she remembered where she now lived. A new start, she reminded herself.

"Franklin," she said quietly, stretching her arm to reach out to her husband. In an instant, she was on her feet, bulldozing through the house.

Trampling up the stairs, without a care for the ungodly noise she was making, she tried to determine how she had managed to fall asleep downstairs. Maybe she had heard a noise, and gone to find out what it was, only for exhaustion to overtake her, causing her to rest on the settee. Or maybe she had gotten up to get herself a drink.

Whatever the reason, she needed to find Franklin. She needed to let him know she was unharmed; she needed to feel safe. He was her safe place and had been since they met. They relied on one another, and it had worked out well – for a short time, at least. Unfortunately, they couldn't always protect one another. If only love could keep people safe.

Sarah burst into the bedroom, relieved to find the love of her life still fast asleep. It was clear he hadn't been disturbed by her going downstairs. Smiling, she walked over to one of her suitcases, removed some clothes, left the room, and headed to the bathroom to get ready for the day ahead.

Not that anything could truly prepare her for what was coming.

Just then, though, she happened to look down. A repugnant grey mark spread from one side of her nightgown to the other, at the knees. How on earth had that that happened? Simply that uncertainty might have sent her into a downward spiral, had she not immediately started the grounding techniques she had learned over the last few months. With studied care, she kept herself from that dire situation she had grown so accustomed to.

In the shower, she revelled in the warmth of the water which left her feeling nothing but peace as the cold left her body. What a wonderful sensation ... water on skin, an experience she had always loved, granted her a happiness she wished she could hold in her hands tightly and never allow it to leave her. But, if every wish was a guarantee, where would we be?

While she was washing, Franklin awoke. Lovingly, he turned to face his wife, to plant a kiss on her cheek to awaken her. Upon noticing his wife's absence, he shakily cried her name.

But then he heard the water crashing through the pipes, and he understood where she was. Keep a clear head, he chastised himself, somewhat irritated. You're supposed to be the strong one. You need to be the strong one. For her. He couldn't crumble. He couldn't make things worse for her. He had to stay strong to keep her together.

CRASH.

Without even deciding to do so, he charged through the house, trying to find the source of that sound.

His feet thundered down the stairs, then he sped straight into the kitchen table and tumbled over a chair. At that moment, a voice spoke his name. He couldn't identify – couldn't imagine – who the voice belonged to. It wasn't one he recognised, and it spoke with a venom that made him shudder with revulsion.

He clambered to his feet. Try as he might, he couldn't remember having moved the kitchen table. He was sure he wouldn't have placed it so close to the stairs.

Assuming he must have moved the furniture while half-asleep, he moved the table once again into the centre of the room, along with the chairs.

He shoved the countless boxes into a cupboard, vowing to deal with them later.

Upstairs, the sounds of Sarah's shower stopped.

Weird, he thought to himself. Everything seems to have moved. Maybe it was Sarah…?

Even as he thought this, he decided the idea was ridiculous. Sarah wouldn't have moved anything without asking him several times where it should be placed: the decision would have worried her. Whenever she asked such questions, her words were daggers in his heart: he wished more than anything he could remove her poisonous anxiety, her self-deprecation. As much as he longed to, though, he knew he couldn't. That knowledge broke his heart. Without him, Sarah's anxiety would never have been triggered.

To know your loved one is suffering, and comprehending the truth that there's nothing you can do to help them or to lessen their suffering … the pain is indescribable, the mental strain is colossal. All one can do is try to understand and do everything one can to keep that person safe.

Sarah cried Franklin's name, and he called back that he was downstairs. Down she came, wearing the most radiant smile he had ever seen. What a gift he had been given to be loved by a woman as smart, as resilient, as brave, as beautiful as Sarah.

"Can you believe I fell asleep down here last night?" she asked.

Screwing his face up in confusion, Franklin replied, "No, you didn't. I distinctly remember you falling asleep in my arms."

"Obviously I needed a drink or something, and dozed off down here."

Franklin looked up at his wife, confused. There was something different about her. Something he couldn't explain or name. "I suppose. Did you sleep well?"

Nodding slowly, Sarah answered, "I don't remember waking up at all in the night, so I guess I did. What about you?"

"I slept like a log," Franklin replied. "What are our plans for today?"

"I'm going to go into town. I'll wander around a bit and get my bearings here. You?"

Franklin considered this as he retrieved two bowls from a box. "I think I'm going to work on my novel. I haven't written in a couple of weeks, and I'd like to get back into it. Would you mind coming back for lunch, and I'll come wandering with you?"

"Okay," was her only response.

Franklin pulled her into his arms, and their lips met. There was something up with her, he knew, but he couldn't decide whether he should ask. A moment or two passed before he settled on letting her tell him when she felt ready.

They sat down to breakfast. Franklin was excited about the prospect of eating. Although they had eaten at The Restaurant less than twelve hours before, their stomachs grumbled, and they salivated at the mere sight of the cereal in front of them.

Outside, the weather seemed to have settled: both the rain and the wind had stopped. However, charcoal-coloured clouds littering the skyline, obscuring any sunlight.

They devoured their meal like starving animals, taking less than five minutes. "I'm not going to lie," Franklin chirped. "That was possibly the best bowl of cereal I've had in my life."

"Yes, me too, actually." Sarah spoke quickly, as though in a rush to get the words out. As Franklin looked at her, smiling lovingly, her eyes widened and began to water. Then, without any warning, she boomed, "I'm leaving," with such volume and venom, Franklin jumped and almost dropped his coffee cup.

Following her outburst, Sarah returned to sipping her own coffee, a soft smile forming on her face. It was as if nothing had happened. She got to her feet.

Beside himself with shock and worry, Franklin asked, "Who were you shouting at? I'm sorry if I upset you." Although he couldn't think what he had done wrong, he clearly had done something. But what?

Sarah raised her eyes to look at her husband. Her eyebrows, and her lips, curved as she answered, "What are you talking about?"

"You just shouted at me with all the might in your lungs," Franklin explained, completely dumbfounded. He didn't know what to do or what to say. He didn't really want to say anything else just in case he upset her further. He fell silent.

His wife stared at him. "I didn't," she said slowly.

Understanding that she genuinely didn't remember, Franklin decided to let it go.

There is definitely something wrong with her, Franklin thought to himself.

He looked at her, standing calmly, drinking her morning coffee, and his heartrate quickened. She was such a beautiful person. He would do anything to keep this woman safe and happy. In spite of the fact he was smiling, he couldn't describe the melancholy that came over him: he didn't know how to help her. If only he'd been slower …

No, he chastised himself.

Having finished their breakfast, Franklin and Sarah cleaned the dishes, and put them away in the cupboards.

"Goodbye," Sarah hissed, marching towards the front door.

"Be safe," he replied.

She closed the door behind her without responding, the thud echoing throughout the house and reverberating in Franklin's skull.

He was alone in the house for the first time. Leaning back against the sink, he surveyed their new home. It could be truly stunning with a bit of updating. As an educated guess, he thought it must have been built in the Victorian era. The furniture was definitely ancient, and was in desperate need of being updated.

There wasn't anything wrong with the furniture. It just wasn't for them. Franklin hoped there would be a charity shop in the town so they could donate it all when they got new chairs, tables and settees.

Happily, at some point in the next few days the internet would be installed, meaning he could continue with the research for his book, and distract himself from what their lives had become.

He made to walk to his study, which he had chosen the night before: the room next to the bedroom.

As he was heading up the stairs, a child's hand slipped into his own. A scream erupted out of him, and he fell backwards. Fortunately, he fell onto the first landing, only a couple of steps below him. Nevertheless, a stabbing pain went up his spine.

Lying there, he chastised himself. What had happened?

Slumped in a heap on the landing, Franklin looked around. This isn't the way things were meant to go: only a year ago, they had been happy beyond description. Now, look at them. He imagined what their lives could have been like, what they should have been, what they would have been. If only life had been kinder to them. "Just keep moving," he said to himself, forcing himself up into a sitting position. He shuffled across the landing, grabbed part of the balustrade, and hoisted himself to his feet.

Then, once more, a child's hand slid into his own. He couldn't explain it. The hand of a child he couldn't see was squeezing his. It was inescapable, inexplicable. Whatever was going on, the presence was pulling at his hand, as though trying to lead him somewhere.

Choosing to ignore the irrationality of his own mind, he continued walking to his study, feeling heavier and heavier with each step he took. He felt as if someone had tied a sack of boulders to his back, and every time he moved, another boulder was shoved in, weighing him down more and more until he couldn't move any further. He tried, and failed, to ignore it. In the end, he gave in, and followed the presence to wherever it would take him.

"Take me where you need me to be," Franklin heard himself say. He wasn't going to fight it any more: this child, this young child he could not see, wanted him to go somewhere. He couldn't let another child down. No, he wouldn't let another child down. "Come on, kid," he said. "Where are we going?"

Nobody answered but, in his head, he heard the following words clear as they could be: "This way."

Following the lead of a child he could not see, Franklin walked back downstairs and through the kitchen. Before he knew where he was, he was standing at the basement door. Though he was unable to put his finger on exactly why he felt this way, he had an overwhelming urge to turn and run away. He would have, too, if only he hadn't felt the need to make the child happy, to not upset the child. He would not let another child down.

Terror flowed through him, mingled with a sense of dread. He knew he shouldn't go down the stairs, though he couldn't understand why. There wouldn't be anything down there but junk, surely.

"You're being utterly absurd," he snapped at himself. Pulling himself out of his trance, he turned to go to his study and finally get some work done.

Chapter Five

Sitting in his study, with all of his papers spread across the desk in an indiscriminate mess, Franklin began to write. Irritated, he stole a glance at his watch, and realised an hour had gone by since Sarah had left, and he hadn't managed to write a single word. How long had he been standing at the top of the stairs to the basement?

As Franklin attempting to immerse himself once again in his novel, his mind worked against him: he couldn't ignore the voice of a child saying, "Come back. Please."

Wait. Is the child crying?

Franklin forced himself not to react or to rise from his seat. He couldn't – no, he wouldn't – allow himself to entertain superstitions. Stay grounded in reality.

But again, the words repeated in his mind. Again. Again. Again.

Studiously, Franklin fought to resist the impulses waging a battle in his head. Every fibre of his being, every instinct, told him to indulge the child, to go to the basement and see what was there. Irrationality? Or curiosity? He wasn't sure. At this point, it didn't matter. He had to be productive. He could not allow himself to be distracted.

Deep within, he knew something was wrong. His brain was acting against itself. He couldn't keep his thoughts straight. One minute he was eager to go with the child, and the very next he was fighting every urge that told him to help the youngster.

You obviously didn't as sleep well as you thought, he told himself, trying to make himself believe his own lies. He knew the truth, though: he had slept better than he had in a long time.

Aggressively, he scribbled words onto the piece of paper in front of him, endeavouring with all his might to ignore the nagging feeling that someone – no, something, not quite human – was watching him. No matter how Franklin tried, he couldn't shake the nagging feeling.

He was struck by an overwhelming need to turn around. He fought the urge, continuing to write, but his resistance dwindled.

Something made him itch to turn around, but something within Franklin told him not to do so. At this point, he knew he was being watched, but was desperately trying to reason with his rampant imagination.

His father's vicious voice came to him, angry and violent. "You'll never amount to anything," his father had told him so many times over the years. "You will be a failure. Always letting your imagination run away with you."

Franklin refused to allow himself to be distracted by the whims of his mind, by the ridiculous thoughts rushing through his head. How could anybody be watching him when he was alone in the house?

Sarah saw a young boy, he remembered. Maybe she wasn't imagining it. Maybe we are not alone.

However, as quickly as these thoughts arose, he dismissed them, remembering the words of his father.

In spite of all endeavours, Franklin knew he wouldn't be able to concentrate until he found assured himself that he was alone. He decided to go and search.

Before he rose from his seat, he counted the lines he had managed to write in the last thirty minutes. The answer: five. Rolling his eyes and groaning in frustration, he thrust himself onto his feet and stomped towards his door.

So lost in irritation, Franklin was completely oblivious to the tapping at the window. If he had heard it, and turned around, he could have saved himself the trouble of searching the house and found evidence of what he tried to dismiss – much quicker.

There, outside his window, was the Janet Baxter, redder than the purest ruby, ready to strike. A cruel smirk curved the corners of her lips. Disappearing into the falling mist, she was formulating a plan to bring her family the safety they needed, they deserved. This, she thought, will take a little longer than before, but the result will be the same.

"You have had your warning," she said.

With that, she became one with the mist.

Franklin stormed downstairs, throwing open door in the house, forgetting to shut them as he searched the house frantically. With every room he entered, his irritation grew, and his frustration deepened. "My imagination," he muttered to himself. Nothing more.

That being said, he was somewhat disappointed with the outcome; for whatever reason, he had hoped to find something. Maybe because he was longing for his distraction to be founded upon something.

What he didn't realise, though, was that as he stampeded through the house, he was being watched by the Baxter family. They looked on in utter fascination as he rampaged around the place. Janet Baxter stared at him, thoroughly satisfied with his frustration.

Time to have some fun with them, she thought. She floated silently and gracefully across the hallway and into the living room, where Franklin was presently peering behind a settee. She moved in perfect synchronisation with him, blowing gently on his neck every so often.

Each time she did so, Franklin would swing around in a fury, waving his arms at the air. The first time, he screamed and fell forwards, shielding his head with his hands like a child. Janet Baxter, feverishly enjoying herself, continued to blow on his neck, and in one instance, she wrapped an arm around him, then watched him squirm like a worm in the mud, not knowing where to move or how to free himself.

Believing he was distracting himself with ridiculous fantasies, Franklin headed back upstairs, gripping the banister with white-knuckled hands to keep from falling backwards. What in the name of sanity, he wondered, is wrong with me today?

He marched back into his study and threw the door shut; its slam echoed through the house and in his head. "Get back to work," he yelled, and took his seat before his desk.

At that moment, everything changed. Suddenly he knew he wasn't alone. He knew someone, or something was in the house with him.

There across several of his papers, in a thick crimson ink, were written the words Get out if you want to live, scrawled in the penmanship of a child – the child who had taken him by the hand. Franklin understood it was a warning, but struggled to deduce the tone. Was it malicious, or pleading?

Franklin had never been one to panic or to become physically anxious, but as soon as he read those words, his body shook like a building at the epicentre of an earthquake. He fell to the floor, trembling. He tried to catch his breath, but couldn't.

What is happening? What is happening? What is happening?

A mere moment later, a crimson spectre stood before him. It watched him, unflinching. Franklin couldn't read the expression on her face. Was she angry? Was she confused? Was she apathetic? Franklin didn't know, and didn't much care: what mattered was that all his life, he had been wrong. This wasn't his imagination. This was real. This was truly happening.

An intense cold swept over him, so bitter he believed he could feel frost forming on his skin. Wailing wind blew through the house, so fiercely that it sent the open cupboard doors flying shut.

Franklin imagined the sound might reverberate through the town as well as the house.

Utilising the grounding techniques Sarah had been taught, Franklin managed to regain control of himself. He clambered onto his seat, resting his head in his hands, leaning on the desk. For a minute or two, he just sat there, resting, his composure returning a little more with each passing moment.

The spectre. He spun around in his chair to find he was, once again, alone in the study. Did I imagine it?

He was unconvinced. It had been so real. The ghost had looked almost corporeal, almost as though she could be touched. But he must have been seeing things. Surely. Ghosts didn't exist.

Before he had time to consider what was real, and what had simply been figments of his imagination, he heard the sound of a child sobbing. He looked around, hoping to see something to substantiate the noise.

Irate at not seeing anything, he called out into the empty hallway, "If someone is there, stop playing these games. Come out. Now."

He pushed himself up onto his feet. Poking his head through the doorway, he looked up and down the corridor. There was nobody there, and he was convinced that he was losing his grip on reality. At the same time, though, he was determined to fight through whatever phase he had entered. This was their new life. This one would not be ruined.

A blast of wind threw Franklin off his feet. With a thump, he landed on his back on the cold wooden floor. Managing to pull himself to the desk, he heaved himself onto his chair. To his shock and horror, he saw that new words had been written. This time, however, they hadn't been scribbled onto his papers, but carved into his desk.

Run away. She is coming.

Franklin couldn't think straight. He couldn't shake the knowledge that they needed to leave the house, for their own safety. He had promised to protect Sarah, and he didn't know how he would do that here. They needed to leave.

But no. They'd spent most of their money on this dreary, forgotten place. They needed to give it a chance. There was very little money left. They didn't have a choice. Thinking about it, neither he nor Sarah had had second thoughts before the purchase was made. Why would they? This was a marvellous house within their budget.

Only now did he realise he should have questioned the estate agent on why exactly a six-bedroom home was so affordable.

Uncertain what his next step ought to be, he simply sat there, going through various scenarios until one thing became clear: he needed to discuss things with Sarah. He knew that, while she possibly wouldn't believe him, she would never ridicule him. But, if he told Sarah what had happened, what reaction would the information cause?

Andrew Lamont

Thinking about it, though, what was there not to believe? The evidence was there, on the papers, on the table, carved as though with a blade.

Who is she?

His ears were ringing, his eyes watering, his entire body shaking. What was going on?

He and his wife had only been here for one night, and already he was second-guessing himself. Although he knew he wouldn't be able to explain away the carving on the table, or the words on his papers, he came to the conclusion that it was his decision what to do about it. He could either let himself be overcome with fear and terror … or, he could just as easily understand somebody was somehow playing a trick on him. He had no idea how this could be, but what was the alternative? Genuine ghosts at play? Ridiculous. Ghosts were not real. Those tales were told by parents to frighten children into behaving: they were not historically or scientifically accurate.

"Yes," Franklin said to himself. "I'm right. There are no such things as ghosts."

Chapter Six

Several hours went by before Sarah walked through the front door, her face aglow and wearing a radiant smile. She bounced into Franklin's study, hopping from foot to foot and, in her excitement, unable to properly string a sentence together or explain to her husband why she was so ecstatic.

"This house," she finally managed, "is where it all started. Our new life together has started, and it's already so much better than what we had before."

She pranced around the study, singing at the top of her lungs.

Deciding against telling her about his traumatic morning, Franklin took her hands in his, and they danced together. They stared with adoration into each other's eyes, just as they had on their wedding day.

As they danced, Franklin hoped that Sarah wouldn't ask questions about his day. If she did, he would have to tell her, and he didn't know how he was going to do so.

Sarah's eyes moved around the room as they continued their dance, and finally fell onto the desk at which her beloved husband had been writing. Without a word, she pulled away from him, dumbstruck at what she had just read. There, carved into the surface of his desk, was a threat.

At once, all colour drained from her face. Her heartbeat hastened, not through anxiety, but through anger. How long had Franklin intended to keep this from her? She understood why he hadn't told her – Franklin would have been panicked about the impact it would have.

Her voice shook as she struggled to contain her numerous emotions. "Do you understand that I don't want you to worry about me? What's going on?"

Dumbfounded, but not yet aware what she was talking about, Franklin looked back at her, not entirely sure what to say, or whether he could have verbalised what he was thinking anyway. After all, what had gone on in that room was nothing short of inexplicable. He couldn't even begin to describe the events without diving into the absurd.

Whatever you do, he told himself, say something.

He could, obviously, lie – though this was something he didn't know how to do. Truth be told, he knew he only had one option. He had to be honest, however ridiculous that may make him sound.

He tried and failed to take Sarah by the hand, then made his way over to the settee at the opposite side of the room. Sarah followed him, standing before him as he sat, glaring down at him with an expression conveying her anger, frustration. "Well?"

"I'm going to tell you the truth," Franklin began, his voice quivering a little. "It's going to sound absurd, but I promise you, my love, this is what happened."

Sarah raised an eyebrow, signalling for him to continue. Although Sarah felt she was as furious as could be, she didn't want to put that theory to the test. She prayed Franklin wouldn't try her patience. She didn't know how much more stress she could take, how much more stress they, as a couple, could take.

Sitting on the settee and staring at the floor, not daring to raise his head to look and see his wife's reaction, Franklin told Sarah the events of that morning in intricate detail, backtracking a few times to make sure he wasn't leaving anything out.

When he had finished the story, Sarah paced around, trying to take in everything she had been told. She understood perfectly why Franklin thought he would sound ridiculous, but even so, she couldn't come to a decision about whether or not she believed him.

She didn't for one second think Franklin had imagined the whole thing, as she may have been tempted to think had it been anybody else telling this story. He had never been the type to let himself be so completely and utterly devoured by indecision and trepidation. She could see it in his eyes: he believed every word he was saying.

She opened her mouth to speak, but then hesitated. Minutes later, she knew what she was going to say. "I understand why you wanted to keep this from me. You were trying to protect me, just like you promised you would. It's a … wild tale, Franklin. But I believe you."

Franklin held his head in his quaking hands. He wasn't even going to answer her. He didn't think she believed him, and he wasn't going to waste his time trying to defend himself if it would mean arguing with the woman he loved.

Seeing the man, she had adored for years trying to hide his distress, Sarah knelt down beside him and took his hands away from his head. Kissing them gently, she repeated, "It's a wild tale, but I believe you."

At once, Franklin's head shot up, and he looked Sarah directly in the eyes. She wasn't lying. She actually believed him. Relief washed over him like a wave. They smiled at one another, and Franklin spoke for the first time in over ten minutes: "Let's go and make some lunch."

In truth, Franklin wasn't hungry, and now neither was Sarah, but he longed desperately to get out of his study. He now knew he hadn't imagined what had happened, and that scared him more than words could say.

Hand in hand, they made their way to the kitchen, dawdling in the corridor and taking their time walking down the stairs. Both wanted to move quicker, but couldn't, for they were walking against a strong wind blowing in from the open window.

Half an hour later, Franklin had made one of the most delicious meals Sarah had ever eaten. Remarkably, given what had happened, he enjoyed it as well. The act of cooking distracted him from his anxieties.

Taking their place at the table, Sarah and Franklin devoured the food. Within five minutes, they had both finished.

"There's clearly something going on in this house. There has to be for you to have seen a spirit. The person – Bradley Taylor - we bought the house from – does he work in the town?""

Franklin's only response was a single nod. He refused to look up, fearing tears would fall.

"In that case, we are going to see him this afternoon. We will not leave his office until we have answers. If this place is haunted, he will know about it. Either way, by dinnertime, we will have the truth."

Just as she finished speaking, the sky cried out in anger as thunder sounded. Then the skies opened, and the rain came down in torrents such as Sarah and Franklin had never witnessed before.

As the storm raged on, without any signs of subsiding, the sound of a singing child came from upstairs. Franklin swung round. Who is upstairs? No, downstairs in the basement. No. Upstairs.

The child – who Sarah guessed could be no older than twelve years old – sang Mary Had A Little Lamb.

Sarah and Franklin's hearts dropped. That was the nursery rhyme they would have sung if … if it hadn't happened. But some things weren't meant to be. Although they understood this, it didn't stop the pain. Sometimes letting yourself drift away to the land of what might have been was easier than living in reality, and easier than trying to come to terms with the most heart-breaking thing that had ever happened to them.

Franklin and Sarah stole glances at one another, and Franklin said, "Let's see what's going on. We stick together. Agreed?"

"Agreed," Sarah replied at once, and was soon halfway across the floor, gaining speed with each step she took.

Refusing to let fear rule over him, Franklin grabbed a screwdriver for protection, and followed his wife. With every second that passed, the singing sounded like it was coming from another room. Whatever was going on, whatever or whoever was in the house, they were taunting them.

With a swift kick, he opened the basement door, flicked the switch and made his way down the stairs. "We're not afraid," he shouted into the room. He cringed as he heard the terror in his voice. As he walked, something breathed on the back of his neck.

Franklin froze. The hairs on his arms stood on end. His breath clouded before him. Employing every ounce of strength in his body, he moved on.

"Maaaaarrrrryyyyyy haaaaaaaaddddddd a llllliiiiitttttllllle laaaaammmmmmb."

The singing grew louder as they descended into the accursed basement. As he walked through the doorway, the singer slowed. Franklin shivered and watched as his breath clouded once again. Hairs prickled on the back of his neck. He was being watched, that much he knew. This time, however, it was as though the person were right in front of him, though he couldn't see them.

A gentle blueish glow caught Sarah's attention, entrapping her in some kind of trance. As she followed it, she felt exceptionally uneasy.

Wandering around upstairs, Sarah opened the door to each room, glancing inside to make sure nobody was there.

When she saw the gentle blue light shining through the bottom of her bedroom door, fear fixed her to the spot. As hard as she tried, she couldn't move. She just stood there, utterly unable to speak, to breathe. They hadn't been alone the night before, and they weren't going to be alone that night.

Sarah felt tears forming in her eyes. Never before had she felt so unsafe, so unable to protect or be protected.

Suddenly, she felt renewed determination such as she had not experienced before. Whatever happened, she was not going to allow fear to reign. She had spent too long being scared. No more.

She opened the bedroom door and walked inside. Immediately, the singing ceased mid-word.

"Please," a voice begged. "Not my children. Please don't hurt my children."

It was the voice of a desperate mother, fearing for her children more than herself. Sarah turned to face the bed, and saw a man hovering over a woman, whose face was drenched in tears. In his hand was a gun, and he appeared set to pull the trigger.

Again, Sarah couldn't move, though she tried with everything she had to do so. She could only watch as the events unfolded. Tears streamed down her face as she watched on, unable to help, to save the woman, or her husband lying next to her, who was already dead. He had been shot in the stomach.

"You will never know what is going to happen to your little brats," the man taunted, a vile grin on his face. "And you will never see them again. Believe me, though, when I say I will take my time with them. They will know you couldn't save them."

As the woman screamed, the monster discharged his firearm, killing her instantly. Blood soaked through the white bedclothes, the pool of red expanding with every passing second. There was nothing Sarah could do to stop any of this.

Having killed the mother and father, the man stalked towards the doorway, and walked straight through Sarah, as though she wasn't there.

She followed him, yelling Franklin's name as she moved, unsure what else to do. She tried to tackle him, but just fell to the ground. Pushing herself back onto her feet, she moved, speedier than she believed she had ever been. However, before she could make it to the children's room, two more shots had been fired, ending their lives.

Without knowing she was about to do so, Sarah let out an almighty scream, letting all the emotion pour unfiltered out of her. Her scream, which was more primal than she could have ever imagined, continued on and on.

Franklin, still searching the basement, heard his wife's anguish. He charged like a bison up the stairs to the ground floor, calling her name every couple of seconds, telling her he was coming and that she was safe. Moving up to the first floor, he yelled her name again. Again. Following the sound of her cries, he found her curled into a ball on the bedroom floor.

Tears stained her cheeks. She rocked back and forth, back and forth, back and forth. Her scream continued, then her voice began to crack, and the screams died down slowly.

Franklin wrapped his arms around her and cradled her as he would a frightened child.

Shushing her soothingly, he held her, not doing anything but being there, protecting her from whatever she had seen, whatever she had witnessed.

Gently, he asked, "What happened?"

His voice, though harsher than he would have liked, was still comforting to Sarah, who continued to rock back and forth, and utilised grounding techniques in a desperate attempt to calm herself down to the point she would be able to speak.

She shook her head, and Franklin knew she was going to take a while to be able to talk again. So, they sat together in the bedroom, holding one another as closely as they could.

"Liiiiiiittttttttttllllllllle laaaaammmmmmmmb, liiiiiittttttttllllllllllle laaaaaammmmmmb."

Franklin heard footsteps coming up the stairs; he held Sarah tighter and braced himself for what was coming. Though he wasn't sure what it was, he knew it would be malicious.

Grinding his teeth, he waited for the whatever was going to appear again.

Thirty seconds later, the singing child appeared in the bedroom doorway. Her curly, bushy hair was tied with a ribbon. Her eyes, sad beyond description, looked into Franklin's. It was then he saw her mouth moving, as though time for her had slowed down. The words came out in a slow, melancholic wail.

Before he was able to form any coherent thoughts, the girl turned and faded away into nothing, leaving the couple alone in the bedroom. Sarah turned to gaze up at Franklin, who didn't look back.

"He …" she began, the word barely more than a whisper, "he just … shot them. As if they were nothing, as if they didn't matter. He showed no emotion. That was all. Look at all the blood on the bed. Look at their bodies."

Franklin furrowed his brow, trying with all his might to see what Sarah was pointing at. All he could see were the green bedclothes they had slept in the night before. There was no blood, and there were no bodies.

Believing she was telling the truth, and hardly in any position to disagree with her, Franklin took the decision to lie. "I see them, Sarah."

"What do we do?" she asked, tears beginning to flow down her cheeks once again. "What do we do? They're gone."

"There's nothing we can do," Franklin replied. "Other than learn what happened in this house, and why all of these things are happening."

Sarah nodded. She knew what must happen next.

Without taking her eyes off the dead bodies lying on the bed like animals in an abattoir, Sarah stood up, defiantly pushing through her fear. She was not going to let them control her. She and Franklin needed answers, and they were going to get them.

They were going to go to the estate agent with fire blazing in them, and they were not going to hold back. The estate agent knew what had happened here, and he hadn't informed them. Everything needed to be explained.

"We're going," Sarah snapped suddenly, the anger in her voice evident. "Now."

Franklin didn't answer, but got to his feet and followed her downstairs.

"When we're there, do not tell me to calm down," Sarah instructed him. "Because I'm not going to."

"I won't," Franklin assured her. "Believe me, I'm not going to tell you to do anything."

"Good."

Having forgotten what she'd seen, Sarah leapt to her feet. Without looking at Franklin, she marched out of the house. Franklin practically had to run to catch up.

Watching them leave, Janet Baxter and her husband smiled.

"When they return," Janet said, "we will truly begin."

Chapter Seven

Coal-black clouds threatened to burst overhead. The rain had stopped, but the wind was strengthening, blowing a gale throughout the town. Nothing would stop them from going to the estate agent's office, and refusing to leave until they had their explanation. Not rain, not snow, not wind, nothing.

They barely spoke to one another as they walked down the hill. Franklin tried, but Sarah didn't seem to hear him. Her determination seemed to have made her deaf. In fact, they hardly even looked where they were going. They just marched, unperturbed by the weather.

Franklin looked around as they made their way into the centre of the town. To his surprise, it seemed that every person there was actively avoiding them, deliberately averting their eyes as they approached.

To his surprise, a young girl wandered up to them to say, "Hello." Her parent pulled her away and more or less ran in the opposite direction. Although it upset Franklin, it didn't seem to bother Sarah in the slightest. As a matter of fact, Franklin wasn't sure if she even noticed. It wouldn't surprise him if she hadn't.

When they finally arrived at the estate agent's office, Sarah burst through the door. She walked up to the receptionist's desk, slammed her hand down on it, and snapped, "We are here to see Bradley Taylor."

The receptionist was clearly taken aback and perhaps even afraid. Trying to keep her voice from shaking, she replied, "Do you have an appointment?"

"No," Sarah replied, in a matter-of-fact tone. "We do not, but we will see him nevertheless."

"I'm really sorry, miss," the receptionist whimpered, "but—"

"We're going to see him with or without your help. We just bought the house at the top of the hill, and—"

"You mean the old abandoned one? The—"

"Yes," Sarah snapped.

The receptionist sat staring at her, wide-eyed. "You should not be here. You have no idea the danger you are putting this town in." She told the couple to follow her, and led them to the personal office of Bradley Taylor. Knocking on the door, she said, "They're here."

Sarah opened the door without waiting for a response, and Franklin followed her in.

Sarah stared at the estate agent with a raised eyebrow, and snapped, "You have some explaining to do. You didn't tell us what was going to happen when we moved into that house."

Bradley Taylor was thinning on top and wore an expensive suit. His face was hard-lined, his eyes severe. He sat looking up at them with frightened eyes, and something resembling shame shadowed his features.

Just from looking at the man in front of him, Franklin could tell he didn't know how to say what he knew he needed to say. He just sat staring at the wall behind them. Gesturing at the receptionist to close the door and leave, he sat up straight, and finally spoke. "I didn't know how to tell you, and I didn't want it to be true. I believed I was doing the right thing."

Shaking her head, her anger bordering on rage, Sarah replied, "You knew exactly what you were doing, and you deliberately hid the truth from us in order to get a sale."

Taylor knew his actions were morally indefensible. Sleep had evaded him the previous night. He had looked at the clock when it read three fifty-one a.m. and he had thought about Sarah and Franklin, what they may have been going through at that moment, less than two miles away. Despite his attempts to get to sleep, his conscience kept him awake. That morning, he had realised he had been crying in the night.

He knew that what he had done was wrong on every level, despite being perfectly legitimate in a business sense.

Bradley Taylor, as everybody who knew him agreed, was a good man who cared profoundly for the people around him. Having done something wrong, he knew what needed to be done.

"I'm sorry," he said. It was the truth, as well.

In fact, that morning he had even considered driving to the house and telling Franklin and Sarah why the house had been so affordable, but he had decided against it. Why? He didn't think he could face them. His nerves and cowardice had held him prisoner in his office.

"Tell us the truth now," Sarah demanded. "We are not leaving until you have told us everything." Her steadfastness was remarkable, given her emotions, but within her mingled fear and fury.

"That place was priced so low due to two reasons," Taylor began. "First, the murders which took place, and second ..."

His voice trailed off, and he looked at them with sad eyes. He wasn't sure how to tell them the second reason.

"Go on," Sarah hissed. She could hear the unfiltered aggression in her voice, but refused to hold back. She had spent too long doing so. "Tell us. You're not getting out of this one."

"The second reason which led to the house cost being so low is because of the stories that have spread about previous owners' ... disappearances."

"What stories?" Sarah demanded, her tone ferocious, her eyes not moving from Bradley Taylor's for a second. Venom flowed through her. Not once, while he was looking at her, did she blink. She would not stand down in any way.

"Five years ago, a family of three moved into that house. A week later, all three of them had sealed themselves away within the house, not leaving once. Less than a week after that, they were dead. Following a long investigation, the verdict was inconclusive. Nobody had any idea how they died, until they found papers in the basement."

"What did these papers say?" Franklin asked. The quaver in his voice wasn't through fear, but rather due to the anger he was trying to subdue. How could Taylor not have told them this?

"They detailed strange experiences with ghosts, with malevolent spirits that sought to kill them all. Even their ten-year-old child. Then the market fizzled out. I wanted to sell the house so we could all move on."

Ghosts. Spectres. Spirits. This is what they had been knowingly sent into. He may have thought he was doing right, Franklin thought, but he was deliberately sending us into danger. He took our money and let us go there.

"And ... those spirits did kill them," Taylor concluded. "They all died, mercilessly slaughtered."

"How could you have sent us in there?" Franklin said. "Why are they doing this?"

"Well, Mister Oswald, the family who initially owned the house was murdered. Shot by Charles Baxter's old business partner. Revenge. The man had been caught stealing money by Charles Baxter. He had said he wanted a raise, and Baxter had told him the company, at that moment, could not afford it. When the man, Lewis Williams, refused to give the money back, and refused to take the offer of a five percent increase of his pay, coming out of Baxter's own pocket, Baxter called the police. Williams was given five years for the continuous thefts.

"He was out two years later because of good behaviour. Mere days after his release, he bought a gun, moved down to the house, and killed the father, the mother, and their two pre-teen children. Without showing any mercy, he shot them in their beds in the middle of the night, and disappeared into the darkness. This was decades ago. The murderer was never found. Now, lingering in the dark, the spirits of the murdered remain. Those parents continue to fight to protect their children. Stories have been around for a long time, but nobody has lived in the house for five years."

"How do you know about the murders? How did the town find out?" Franklin asked. His heart throbbed in pain for the family, the tragedy they experienced, and continued to experience even now.

Tears formed in the estate agent's eyes. "Two days after the murders, the townspeople grew concerned for the family's welfare, as nobody had seen them. Three of Baxter's employees went up to the house and found their dead bodies. They were utterly traumatised and two took their own lives. Within a week of finding the Baxters, they were either dead, or a mere shadow of their previous selves."

Sarah's weeping had become almost uncontrollable. Through strangled breaths, she said, "I saw the man – Williams - kill the parents. Well, Janet Baxter," she corrected herself.

Bradley Taylor's eyes widened, and he gasped.

"He taunted her before killing her, and I understand why she wants to protect her child."

"Sarah," Franklin chimed in, turning in shock to look at his wife. He reached out to take Sarah's hand, but she refused to offer it.

"No, it's time to speak about it," she replied without turning to face her husband. "We lost a child. If we had had that baby, I would do whatever I had to do in order to protect her from any perceived threat."

Bradley Taylor completely missed the point. "What do you mean?"

"I mean," Sarah continued, angered by his idiocy, "that the parents believe we are a threat to them, and their children. It is, therefore, up to us to prove we are not there to harm them. What you have just told me has proved to me beyond any doubt that the last person they had in their home during their lifetime was a threat. The beast murdered them all. I'm saying that I understand the mother's standpoint. In future, just a quick tip: do not keep things from those to whom you are selling a house."

With that, Sarah stood and marched out of the room without saying another word. Franklin followed her.

After they had left, the real estate agent broke down in a fit of tears so violent that his body shook.

***

As they walked through the town, neither Sarah nor Franklin could verbalise their thoughts. Nevertheless, they both knew where they were going: the library.

As had been the case earlier, everybody in the town avoided them. Something was different now, though. Nobody was trying to hide the fact that they were deliberately keeping their distance from them. What was more, Franklin no longer cared. What he cared about was clearing all fear from the family who had owned that house. He understood the love parents have for their children.

Though he and his wife had never met their own child, Sarah loved her with all of her heart. Although she had never heard the girl's voice, she missed what they had never had. Although she had never seen her face, she longed to kiss her cheek. More than anything, though, Sarah wished she could have protected the child.

They marched through the town centre to the library, not even stopping to ask for directions as they had studied the map before the move.

Franklin was the first to break the silence. "What do we need to find out?"

Without turning to face him, Sarah replied, "We need to find out how to summon the family. We know they fear us to the point of going on the offensive, and we need to tell them they have no need to be frightened. The whole point of parents is to protect their children and that is what they are trying to do. When we summon them, we will put their minds at rest, as well as protect ourselves from their hatred."

The library was made up of darkened bricks, blackened by the elements. Neither Franklin nor Sarah could see through the windows, but they didn't much care. All they wanted to do now was learn what they needed to know.

Inside the building, they made a bee-line for the customer desk, and Franklin made himself ask the following question as calmly as he could: "Where is the non-fiction section on the supernatural?"

Looking up with a radiant Cheshire Cat grin that irritated Sarah to no end, the woman behind the desk said, "If you go through those two doors, take a right, go up the stairs, and take a left, it will take you to the supernatural section."

Thanking her, Franklin and Sarah sped towards the doors, so determined that they didn't hear the receptionist calling after them, begging them not to go back to that house and to leave the town.

They climbed the stairs two steps at a time.

In the supernatural section they went in different directions, both hoping they would discover whatever it was they needed to know. The room was huge, the book collection extensive.

Franklin and Sarah dived deep into their research. Hoping desperately to find something they could use to keep the peace, they read countless pages, spending hours in the library. This was nothing unusual for them: they had both held Masters degrees. However, they had never needed to do research in this particular area, and so everything they read was new to them.

After several hours had passed, Franklin found what they were looking for.

Holding a weighty tome, he walked around the library floor in an attempt to locate his wife. When he finally found her, he said, "Sarah, look at this. To summon a ghost, we need a circle of twelve candles, with a symbol of joy in the centre."

Dumbfounded, Sarah read the page over and over again before asking the question Franklin hadn't wanted to ask: "What is a symbol of joy?"

Franklin shook his head. "I really don't know."

"A symbol of joy is the object you love the most," came a deep, solemn voice from behind them, causing them both to spin around in fright. The man the voice belonged to was elderly, and clearly starting to fail: he held onto bookcases for support. "For example, for my mother I'm sure it would be my birth certificate. It reminded her of what she called her greatest accomplishment. Whatever it is, it is the first thing that came to your mind when you heard me speak."

"Our wedding rings," Franklin and Sarah said together. Although curious as to the man's identity, they weren't interested enough to ask: they had other priorities.

"If that's what you love the most," the strange man snarled, before stalking away into the shadowed corners of the room.

"That's what we need to do then," Franklin declared. "Do we still have the candles your mother and father gave us for our wedding?"

Sarah shook her head. "We burned them last year during the blackout," she said, irritated.

"It doesn't matter," Franklin said. "We can buy more. We just go to shop around the corner, and buy twelve of the cheapest ones on the shelves. And matches, of course," he added, smiling at Sarah, who half-smiled back. He went to return the hefty volume to its shelf.

After putting the book back where Franklin had found it, they left the library. Rain had started to hammer down with a hitherto unprecedented ferocity.

Making their way across the idyllic town square, Franklin and Sarah knew they were journeying into dangerous territory: they were going to summon the Baxters.

The little shop they entered was filled with so many candles that an intoxicating mix of different scents which created an assault on the senses.

As they opened the door, a bell rang above their heads. Franklin called across the shop to the woman standing behind the counter, "What is your cheapest candle?"

The woman behind the desk was somewhat severe and angry-looking. She pushed herself to her feet, sending her chair toppling to the floor.

"You ask me what the cheapest candle in my shop," she said, her voice cold and emotionless but her eyes ablaze. "Let me have you know, young boy, I have no cheap candles. Only candles low in price, but they not cheap."

"Which candle is the lowest in price?" Franklin demanded, hoping not to anger her further – not least because it occurred to him that she might well have voodoo dolls in the back of her shop, and he'd rather not have one of them used against him.

"Candle lowest in price," the woman muttered, pondering the question as she looked around her quaint little shop. Walking stiffly as though on stilts, she moved across to a set of yellow candles. "These ones. These ones low. Five pounds each."

"We'll take twelve," Sarah insisted. "Twelve candles."

The woman seemed shocked by the quantity. She turned her head to stare at each of them in turn. "You think twelve enough?" she snapped.

"That's the number I said," Sarah said. "The purchase comes to sixty pounds, yes?"

The woman nodded curtly and got the order ready. "You know number," she hissed, holding her hand out for the money, her lips pursed. Sarah handed over the cash, and Franklin took the candles. "Now, leave shop," the woman demanded. "Only return to buy more."

Franklin followed Sarah to the exit. They were fast approaching the point of no return and they didn't even know it.

Chapter Eight

As the rain poured unrestrained around them, Franklin and Sarah held hands as they walked into the grounds of their new house. Franklin looked at Sarah as they were about to enter the house, utterly terrified at the mere thought of losing her. He had to keep her safe.

"You know," he said, not even sure what was about to come from his mouth, "I love you more than words could ever even come close to expressing. Before we met, I was half a person, surviving but not living. Meeting you was the best thing that has ever happened to me. You make me whole, and I can never thank you enough for that."

Sarah let go of the door handle, caressed his face with her hands, leaned in and kissed him. "I love you, too, Frank. Whatever I did to deserve meeting you, I am so relieved I did it. The best gift I have ever received was you, and I know with all my heart, all my being, that I want to be with you for the rest of my life."

They embraced, and their lips met. At that point, they entered their house. "Are you ready?" Franklin asked Sarah, not entirely certain if he himself was. Sarah nodded. "Let's do it," he said.

At once, an angry wail sounded somewhere in the house – Franklin and Sarah understood that the family knew of their presence. A violent cold seeped into their bodies.

In spite of the fact that nobody had told them where to conduct the summoning, Sarah had a strong inclination that it ought to be in the living room. Why? Simply because it was the largest room in the house.

Reluctantly, Franklin and Sarah entered the living room and spread out the candles in a circle, as they had read about. Pulling the box of matches out of his pocket, Franklin said to Sarah, "Whatever happens, I love you."

"Don't talk like that," Sarah replied. "We are going to succeed. When the family see that we're not bad people, we can live in peace, and they can rest."

"Okay," Franklin replied. He took off his wedding ring and Sarah did the same. In one swift motion, Franklin struck a match and started lighting the candles one by one, moving slowly around the circle. The daylight outside was retreating, giving way to creeping dark. Before Franklin had even finished lighting the candles, they were in a sea of black. No moonlight shone that night.

All the candles were now lit. There was no going back.

"Spirits, we summon you," Sarah said, her voice calm and cold.

Pans clattered and clanged; plates fell out of cupboards, shattering as they hit the floor;

glasses fell to the ground with a crash; the candle flames, which had once been still, shook and swayed as though in wind; furniture screeched as it moved across the floor. Settees scratched their way across the floor, vases fell to the ground and smashed, chairs were upended.

"Something's here," Franklin whispered, false bravado veiling the fear in his voice.

The flames of the candles connected to form a ragged circle of fire. Franklin squinted at the sudden flash of light. When he opened his eyes, before him were the Baxters.

Franklin stepped back, almost falling over a footstool which had moved from its original position. Janet Baxter was an odd shade, flickering between orange and blue; the father likewise. Their children, however, were baby blue. Held by terror, they clung onto their parents.

"Why have you come here?" the mother asked, her ostensibly pleasant tone fooling no one. She turned crimson as she spoke. For some reason, her tone didn't seem to intimidate Sarah, though Franklin was sure it would have.

Clearly growing angrier, the mother repeated her question. Sarah stared her adversary directly in the eye. She would not allow herself to be afraid.

Following a moment's silence – apart from the rain outside – Sarah spoke. "We came here after we lost our child. Franklin and I wanted a new start, a new beginning. We chose this place so we could navigate our new normal without commentary from anyone else." As she contemplated how to word her next sentence, a single tear rolled down her cheek. That day, she had referred to her miscarriage twice. Before this point, she hadn't spoken of the tragedy even once.

Upon seeing her tears, Franklin took the opportunity to speak. "Sarah and I heard what happened to your family, to you and your two wonderful children. We understand some what you went through because we went through the loss of a child, and continue to this day to endure that pain. It's natural that you want to protect your children. But Sarah and I promise you that we pose no threat to you or your children. Neither of us want to harm you. We don't want to harm anyone. We just want to live our lives. Quietly."

The mother's expression hardened, her fists clenched and the veins in her arms flared, pulsing through her skin. "I decide who is and who is not a threat to my family. You have until sunrise to leave, or you will face the consequences. I promise you, they will be severe."

Sarah stepped forward. Droplets of sweat moistened her brow and desperation made her eyes glimmer. "Please," she pleaded. "Give us a chance to prove to you we would never deliberately harm anyone, especially not you or your children. We would never do such a thing. We will not be leaving."

After a moment's thought, the mother's face softened, and she looked almost kind. "Very well," she said, and at once the flames extinguished. All spirits left, leaving Franklin and Sarah in darkness.

For a while they stood there, motionless. The conversation, they both thought, had gone as well as could have been expected. How wrong they were!

***

The evening passed without anything of note occurring. Sarah sat in the living room trying to read her favourite classic novel – Great Expectations, but try as she might, she couldn't stop thinking of the child she should be holding at that moment, the child they would never hold. Franklin was sitting beside her, writing more of his novel, finally able to concentrate.

A fire crackled in the grate, its heavy heat filling the room. Outside, the wind howled, and rain poured.

Hours went by as they sat quietly, focusing on their novels. Before they knew it, the clock chimed eleven. Franklin looked at Sarah, who had fallen asleep on the settee beside him, her book still open to the page she had been reading. He didn't want to wake her up, but at the same time, he didn't want to leave her here alone.

So, he went to the cupboard in the hallway and removed a sleeping bag they had last used when they had gone camping the day after they had graduated university. Looking back on that time was a blessing: they had been so happy, so carefree. So unaware of what was coming.

He covered Sarah with a blanket, then climbed into his sleeping bag. Before the clock struck again, he was sound asleep, dreaming of the camping trip, dreaming of when he was happy.

***

As the rain continued to fall and the wind continued to cascade against every wall of the house, the spirit of Janet Baxter watched Franklin and Sarah sleep. They looked so peaceful, so tranquil, so harmless. But she knew better than to trust people. She had trusted before, and it had cost her dearly. Never would she make that mistake again. Never would she put her beloved children in danger again. Never.

The sun was beginning to rise, which meant their time was up. Generously, she and her husband had given the couple a chance to get their things together and get out of their home. Foolishly, they had squandered that opportunity, and now they would suffer for it.

It was obvious they loved one another. But, as Janet well knew, love was not enough to save someone. If it was, this story would have been very different.

However, Janet didn't act in that moment. She just watched the people who had strode into her home. There wasn't a doubt in her mind that they truly believed themselves to be good people. Unfortunately for them, she knew the depths of evil in their hearts, and she would not let her children suffer anymore.

She would make her move sooner rather than later. Her promise to the couple would be carried out. As she had told them, the consequences for their choice would be severe. She would show no mercy. Graciously, she had offered them an escape; they had denied it. Now, they would pay dearly. Just like she had.

They have a nerve, she thought, anger bubbling through her. They marched into my home, and they tried to manipulate me. They tried to tell me I was overprotective. Oh yes, they are going to suffer.

After deciding exactly how she was going to carry out her intentions, Janet stalked away, fading away into shadows to became one with the darkness.

Chapter Nine

Slowly but surely, the sun rose, shining through the wasteland that was Franklin and Sarah's garden. The relentless light awoke Sarah first, and she looked around, momentarily disoriented. Where am I?

Then she saw the sun rising above the trees. Relief washed over her. The family had kept their promise, and had believed her and Franklin. Thank goodness, Sarah thought. They were going to be able to begin to rebuild their lives, something they hadn't been able to do – but not through a lack of trying. Finally, they could begin again.

As she got to her feet, she was hit by a sense of overwhelming emptiness. Walking up the stairs, she understood why: it had happened six months before. Six months had gone by since they had lost their beautiful girl. Empty, void of feelings, numb. Making her way into her bedroom, she walked straight to her bag, and searched for the sonogram.

Sarah had been priding herself for not looking at the sonogram, giving herself credit for trying to move on. Still, she knew she would never be the way she had been before her pregnancy. For as long as she lived, there would always be a void that would never – could never – be filled.

Today, though, things were different. It had been six months.

They had discussed trying again. Once. However, neither of them could face the thought of it happening all over again. In the end, they decided against it.

As horrible as it sounded to her, she looked forward to the day when she could look back and feel nothing but love. No self-loathing. That day was her goal. It would come, she knew. But when it might come, she had no idea.

"You will never understand how much you mean to me," she said. "You will never know how much I miss feeling you close to me, as close as anyone could be to another. I love you, and I'm sorry we never met. I'm sorry you were never born."

Before the tears came, she walked away from her handbag, walked to the closet, pulled out a towel, and headed through to the bathroom to shower and get ready for the day ahead. Not that anything could have prepared her for what was coming.

As the warm water poured over her, cleansing her of the events of the day before, she attempted to consider what new things this day would bring. Try as she might, she could only think about the end of the day, the point when she could curl up under the covers and dream of how things had been, dream of what could have been.

That was when it hit her: she hadn't even seen the sonogram in her bag. Turning the water off, she dried herself and threw some clothes on.

Quick as she could, she moved through the house and into the bedroom. Turning her bag upside-down, she emptied it. The sonogram was not there.

Sarah, raking through the cupboard for the sonogram, allowed the tears to freely flow down her face. It was always in her bag. She would never leave it anywhere else. Her beautiful baby. She had lost it twice now.

I wish my Grandmother was here, Sarah Oswald thought to herself, leaning back onto her feet, the flow of tears increasing.

Just then, in a corner shrouded in shadow, she saw a box. In spite of the unrelenting mass of dust settled upon everything else, none coated that corner. Scrawled on the side of the box facing her were the following words: The Beyond.

Out of interest, she pulled the box out from the cupboard and into the bedroom. Opening it, she thrust herself backwards, careening into the foot of her four-poster bed. Destroy it. Destroy it. Destroy it.

Again and again, she instructed herself to get that thing out of the house. No good can come from dabbling in that which you do not understand. All she knew of these things was that they were evil.

Through impulse, nothing more, she opened her mouth to scream Franklin's name. As she was about to call on him, another thought came into her mind. Every ounce of fear she had been experiencing disappeared in an instant.

I can speak to Grandma, she realised. She will know what to do.

Sarah had grown up in a somewhat spiritual family. Although she wasn't sure how to use the wooden plank laying in front of her, Sarah knew exactly what it was: a Ouija board. Her parents had always warned her against using one, claiming they were the embodiment of malice and evil. Most of all, she was warned to always say Goodbye.

Once more, Sarah wanted to shout on her husband, but she didn't: Franklin would never agree to using the powerful portal and would almost definitely try and stop her from doing the same.

Moving forward to remove the board from its box, a vile chill seeped into Sarah's body. A warning, perhaps? A coincidence? Whatever was happening, Sarah would not be stopped. Sarah picked it up and removed it. At once, a crashing thump sounded from downstairs. Regardless, Sarah continued, not even noticing the light flickering above her head.

After placing the board on the floor, Sarah searched in the box for the planchette. She wasn't surprised when she didn't find it: common knowledge dictates one should always keep the board and planchette separate when not in use.

Making to stand up, she felt a breeze sift through her body, and heard a voice telling her not to turn around. Whoever was speaking to her did not elaborate. Though she didn't know why, she was pretty certain it was Janet Baxter.

A slight movement of the head angered the presence. "I said," it hissed, "do not turn around. For when you do, you will die."

"What do you want?" Sarah asked, struggling to keep her voice from shaking.

No answer came, and so Sarah turned around.

When she saw she was alone, she rolled her eyes. After the nightmare she had had, Sarah wasn't surprised that her mind had started working against her.

Her eyes dropped to the floor where the Ouija board sat. There, on top of it, sat the planchette. I must've missed it, Sarah concluded, sitting down.

Moving it around in a circle once, Sarah said, "Is there anybody here?"

Andrew Lamont

Another crash from downstairs told Sarah she wasn't alone. Making to close the door, Sarah went to move, but couldn't. She couldn't describe what was happening, or what was keeping her in place. All she understood was this: no matter how she tried, something was holding her down.

Her hand moved. Her eyes followed the planchette as it centred itself on the board. "Grandma, is that you?" she asked, her voice breaking under the strain and pull of her emotions.

Nothing happened.

"Grandma, are you there?" Sarah asked again. "I miss you. Please speak to me. Are you there?"

Scratching across the board, the wooden triangle moved. Yes.

Sarah shivered as the temperature in the room dropped. Another tear fell from her eye. "There's so much I wish I could tell you."

No movement – only the creaking of a floorboard behind Sarah. Not that she heard it. An ice-cold breath fell onto the back of Sarah's neck. Her hairs stood up on end, but she was still unaware. Poor Sarah Oswald wasn't even aware of the door she had just opened; nor was she aware of the spirits lingering in the darkness, staring at her.

"You were so wise. Always knew what advice to give me." Sarah continued to tell whatever spirit she had contacted about what was happening in the house, how lost she felt. How unsure she was of what to do. "What do I do, Grandma?"

R-U-N

"What do you mean?" she replied. "Run where?"

R-U-N

Through gritted teeth, Sarah snapped, "Where?"

Y-O-U W-I-L-L D-I-E I-N T-H-I-S P-L-A-C-E A-N-D T-H-E-N, T-H-E-N Y-O-U W-I-L-L B-E M-I-N-E

At once, Sarah, knowing this was not her grandmother, kicked the board away. Not wanting to hold the planchette any longer, she threw it into the closet, and kicked the Ouija in after it. Slamming the door, Sarah promised herself she would never use one of those again.

She wouldn't need to.

The damage was done.

Sarah had not said Goodbye.

That door to the unknown was still open.

A crucifix had once hung on the closet door, but now, it lay on the floor.

All protection was gone.

Downstairs, Franklin was just beginning to stir and wake up. He hadn't slept particularly comfortably. When he tried to stand up, his back cried out. A shooting pain forced its way up his spine.

In retrospect, he should have slept on the other side of the settee – as opposed to the wooden floor, but he hadn't wanted to disturb Sarah: she had had such a trying day, she deserved the rest she got, and probably more. Franklin hoisted himself onto the settee, and stretched out, soothing the pain in his spine.

He looked out the window and, seeing the rays shining through the trees, released a breath he hadn't realised he was holding in. Nothing had happened. They were fine – or, at least, as close to 'fine' as they could ever be. The Baxters had believed them. Franklin felt indescribably relieved.

In the bedroom, fighting to keep a handle on her trembling body, Sarah moved at speed across the room, into the corridor and down the stairs. "I'm going to the cathedral," she told Franklin, without explaining.

Before he could reply, Sarah was out of the door.

***

Within seconds, Franklin's nerves started to play up.

Janet Baxter had been so against them, and their being in this house. Those threats had not been empty, and Franklin did not trust that the peace would last long. In fact, he knew it wouldn't. Janet Baxter's malice had disappeared too quickly, too easily. You do not lose the hatred you have held for decades in mere moments.

What could they do?

Minutes went by, in which Franklin thought desperately about what they could do to get out of the house, where they could go … even if only for a day or two.

Then it hit him: there was a hotel in the town. For two nights, they would stay there. What else could they do? Staying in that house right then, when the danger was so high, was nothing short of a gamble with their lives.

He walked up the stairs and into their bedroom to dress. Quickly, he threw into a bag enough clothing to last him three days. He didn't pack anything else. From there, he sat and waited.

***

Rushing down the hill with all the speed she could muster, Sarah couldn't help but feel something was very, very wrong. There was something she had forgotten, though she couldn't think what had slipped her mind.

Without stopping once for breath, she galloped through the town, bursting into the cathedral. No tears stained her face; she had gone past the point of fear, and was now imprisoned by terror. She was alone.

In spite of her adolescent reluctance to pray, Sarah felt it was all she had left to do. Not truly believing anybody would be there to listen, she sat down in a pew, and closed her eyes.

Before Sarah had a chance to open her mouth to begin her plea for help, a deep voice spoke from behind her. "You should not have come here," it said, stern but not angry. "This is the house of our Lord."

Turning around, Sarah opened her eyes to see a woman dressed in all white. A future nun who had not yet given her vows, she believed. With eyes which betrayed wisdom beyond her years, the woman stared at Sarah, unblinking.

Clutching the crucifix hanging around her neck, the nun stood perfectly still.

"I'm sorry," Sarah began, not sure what she was apologising for. "I don't know where else to go."

After taking a single step back, the nun said, "You are a dark beacon. I sense deep darkness surrounding you. You should not be here. You have to leave. Now."

Sarah shook her head, and forced herself to her feet. In front of her, the nun stood still. That is, until Sarah started walking towards her with her hands closed as if in prayer. "Please," she begged. "Help me."

Relenting slightly, a shadow of regret crossed the nun's features. "There is nothing I can do. You have opened a door which must never be open. You have communicated with evil."

The Ouija Board, Sarah realised. In that moment, Sarah remembered what she had forgotten: she had not said Goodbye. That communication was still open. What had she done?

"What do I do?" Sarah asked.

"You have been marked," the nun said, almost in surrender. "There is nothing you can do." She turned to walk away, but stopped. "Wait outside."

Sarah obeyed and, with that, the nun entered another room.

Standing outside, all Sarah could do was watch as the people around her stayed as far away as they could. She was alone in an ocean of darkness. Nobody could help her. Even if they could, she doubted any of them would. They knew of the hatred encapsulating that house.

A mere couple of minutes went by and the nun returned. In her hand, she held two things: a crucifix, and a small coloured bottle containing liquid of some description. Confused, Sarah said nothing.

"These will keep you safe," the nun said. "Only use this holy water as a last resort."

She placed the items into Sarah's open hands. Before Sarah could thank the woman, she was out of sight.

That, however, was the least of Sarah's worries: she had left the portal open, and Franklin was still in that house.

***

Upon walking away from the church, Sarah felt her stomach sink. Regardless of the fact that she could see no-one whenever she turned around, Sarah could feel the eyes of something inhuman following her, watching her.

Picking up speed, Sarah kept moving. As she ran through the town, all townspeople in the streets cleared a path for her, avoiding eye contact by any means. Not that she cared. The only thing she cared about now was getting to Franklin and getting him out of that house. How could she have been so stupid as to not end the communication properly?

She should never have used that accursed board. Who could fathom what sort of evil she had allowed to be unleashed?

Above Sarah's head, the sky darkened. Grateful for the sun which lit her path – at least somewhat, Sarah ran towards the house.

Once again, that horrendous feeling of being watched overwhelmed her. Fighting every fibre of her being, every instinct which told her to turn around, Sarah tried to keep moving. As she grew closer to the house, the feeling strengthened and strengthened.

Unable to suppress the urge any longer, Sarah turned around. Stumbling backwards, and falling over a rock, she tried to get away from the silhouetted figure in front of her.

Whoever it was, their face was completely obscured by their hood. In fact, every feature of their body was hidden by the cloak the person wore.

Sarah was about to speak, but the figure crossed its arms into an X, silencing her. It didn't matter how much she attempted to move, to speak. She couldn't do anything but watch and listen. As it turned away from her, the moon disappeared behind a cloud.

"Sarah Oswald," the figure said, its voice deep, husky and perfectly inhuman. "We are many while you are few. For too long, we have been trapped in there. Now, we are released. She lives. She watches. She kills."

Something scurried across her hand, causing a scream to build up within Sarah. In the time it took her to blink, the figure had vanished, and the sunlight had returned.

At once, she was on her feet and sprinting up the hill towards that house. Relieved, Sarah saw a light on in the bedroom. As she ran past her car, something caught her eye. Looking back, it was made clear: something else was there.

Scratched onto her car, as though with a rock of some description, were three sixes, surrounded by flipped crosses.

Suppressing a scream, she burst into the house, and yelled her husband's name with all the might she could muster.

When he didn't answer, she sprinted across the floor to the stairs, hammered up them, and into the bedroom. Though relieved to see Franklin sitting on the bed, completely unharmed, his almost colourless complexion caused her to stop dead in the doorframe.

Paler than the dead, Franklin remained still, his hand holding a book of some kind. Regardless of his clear attempts to hide the fact, Sarah knew he had been crying.

"We need to leave," she said. "Now."

Franklin gave her no response. As a matter of fact, had he not flinched when she spoke, Sarah would have questioned whether he had noticed her presence.

Without speaking, he lifted the book toward her, signalling for her to read it. Taking it from his hand, she didn't blink once. Though she couldn't explain it, or describe exactly what it felt like, as she held that book, a sensation of emptiness, of hollowness coursed through her.

Flicking it open, she saw what Franklin had: their names, their birthdates, and their causes of deaths.

Franklin Oswald – born on the eighteenth day of the month of December, 1990. Died on the sixth day of March, 2008. Cause of death: broken neck after falling from a height.

Sarah Oswald – born on the ninth day of the month of June, 1991. (Presumed) Died on the sixth day of March, 2008. Cause of death: Unknown. Body was never recovered.

"We are leaving," Sarah repeated through gritted teeth, her voice shaking along with her body. "Now. Get up. We are going. We will not be dying tonight."

Sarah, refusing to wait for a reply, threw as many clothes into a bag as she possibly could.

When she turned around again, Franklin was on his feet.

Mere seconds later, they were leaving.

***

They passed straight through their house and out of the grounds, where the sun beat down on them. In Britain, whenever the sun shone it felt like a blessing. In normal circumstances, they would have enjoyed the sunlight on their faces, revelled in the heat. However, today the rays did nothing but obscure their vision, leaving them vulnerable to attack. Anxiety rose within each of them.

Early morning should have brought with it the singing of birds, but today there was no singing. There are some places even birds avoid, Franklin thought to himself. Thinking about it, neither Franklin nor Sarah had seen one since they moved into that manor house. What was it about that place that frightened even the birds?

As they made their way down the hill leading to the town, Franklin frowned. He couldn't shake a question from his mind: Is the mother evil, or desperate? As far as he was concerned, there was a stark difference between the two. Desperate people do evil things, but they are not inherently vicious. Evil people, however, ... that was something different entirely.

He asked Sarah for her opinion.

The answer came to her. "In all honesty, I don't think anybody has the right to kill anybody else in cold blood."

Franklin shot back, "What about killing someone in self-defence?"

Sarah shook her head, turning to look at her husband. "Self-defence is self-defence, there's no getting around that."

The couple spent the rest of the walk to the hotel in absolute silence, neither wanting to talk to the other, neither really knowing what they would say if they were to speak. Above them, the clouds were clearing, and the sun was shining, its glare growing more and more aggressive with each passing second.

When they arrived, the hotel receptionist began speaking before looking up. "Welcome to The Village Hotel. My name is Rachel. t. We hope we can make your stay as pleasant as possible." Her tone was soft – but when she looked up her demeanour changed. "What are you doing here?" she asked, her voice laced with fear and anxiety. "Why have you come here?"

Franklin, somewhat taken aback, couldn't think of anything to say other than, "Please. We just need a room."

"Why have you come here?" the receptionist repeated, her hands shaking as she raised them to push back the hair that had fallen in front of her face. "Do you know what you have done?"

"How do you even know who we are?" Sarah demanded.

"You have the paleness of one who has seen her."

"Please," Franklin pleaded. "We don't have anywhere else to go. If we did, we wouldn't have come. All we need is a room for a night, to get away from them for a couple nights. We saw her, spoke to her. She is giving us a chance."

The receptionist, Rachel, shook her head. Her eyes watered, and she fought to keep tears from falling. "Y-y-you," she stammered, struggling to regain her composure. "You can never get away from her now."

"Why?" Sarah asked. "What is so special about us?"

"You say you have seen her?" Rachel questioned. Sarah could only nod in response. The receptionist grabbed Sarah's hand. "I'm sorry, miss," she wept. "If you have seen her, she has marked you. It's not the house she's interested in. It's the people who enter it. You have brought danger to this hotel."

"What can we do?" Franklin asked, his voice calmer than he felt. Every part of his being was fighting to keep himself from breaking down in hysterics.

"It doesn't matter what you do," the receptionist explained. "I mean … have you spoken to her?"

Franklin nodded. He stepped forward, putting his hand on the desk. "Yes, we have. She said she would give us a chance to prove we are not dangerous people."

The receptionist stared at him, incredulous. "How do you propose to prove something like that?" she snapped. "What else did she say?"

"She said she would give us until sunrise to get out, or we would face the consequences. But that was before she gave us the chance."

"No," the receptionist said, her tears flowing unhindered down both cheeks. "She lied to you, if that's the case. I'm sorry. You cannot escape her wrath. Her hatred is too strong. And … and she is too powerful."

"This is the only hotel in town. Please," Sarah pleaded.

Turning her back on the couple for a moment, the receptionist took a key from the small cupboard behind the desk, muttering a silent prayer for Franklin and Sarah, herself, and the town. None of them were safe if she allowed them to stay here, but she couldn't let them go back to that house. So, the receptionist did the only thing she knew she could do in this circumstance: her job.

"Room four-twenty-six," she whimpered. "God be with you." Instantly, regret clouded her features.

Sarah took the key from the receptionist, thanked her, and she and Franklin set off to find the room.

When they were out of sight, the receptionist broke down in tears. "Have mercy on us," she pleaded. We will never know if she was pleading with God, or the mother of those murdered children. Maybe that's for the best. What we know is distressing enough. What was about to happen is horrifying enough.

Eventually, Franklin and Sarah found the room they had been assigned. Upon closing the door, they collapsed onto the bed and stared up at the ceiling, trying not to think about what their lives had become. What they didn't know, though, was that their lives were about to become darker than ever.

Chapter Ten

Sitting there in the hotel room, unsure what to do with themselves, not sure how to even function, Sarah and Franklin were silent for what felt like an eternity.

"How do we protect ourselves?" Sarah asked. "We have no idea what we are up against. We do not know anything about it."

"That's it!" Franklin exclaimed.

Sarah looked at her husband, waiting for him to elaborate and explain his outburst.

"We cannot protect ourselves from something we know nothing about," he said.

His words had the opposite impact he had thought they would. "Thanks for that ground-breaking discovery," Sarah hissed, and thrust her head back onto her pillow.

Ignoring his wife's saltiness, Franklin continued, "Do you not see? All we need to do is go to the library. We looked into the summoning of spirits. What about repelling them?"

Sarah jumped to her feet. "Let's go."

A minute later, they were running through the hotel. As they sped down the stairs, into the hotel reception and out of the door, Sarah said, "You go to the library. I'm going to the cathedral. Maybe there will be some somewhere that could help us somehow. Or maybe the priest can help."

They went their separate ways, each with a determination they hadn't had before, a desperation they hoped they would never have again.

***

The church's cone-shaped turrets stretched far higher than seemed necessary, in Sarah's opinion. Organised religion had always been an odd thing for her, though she wasn't sure why.

The mere thought of entering this cathedral made her incredibly uneasy. She hadn't been inside a church since her mother's funeral. That being said, the thought of not going in made her feel wrong, too.

The moment she set foot inside the building, she was overwhelmed by a feeling she couldn't describe, a feeling she had never had before. It was absolute peace. Safety. Sarah looked up to the roof, and noticed the almost abnormal amount of gold strewn around it.

She walked around the sanctuary, looking around for something, anything that might help her in some way. When she didn't, she sat down in a pew in despair.

Unable to contain her emotions, she started sobbing. Her cries sounded throughout the cathedral, and came to the ears of the priest. He wasn't at all surprised to see Sarah – the woman he had heard about via the gossip in the pews, and the nun, the woman who had moved into that house – sitting in his church once again.

"My child, how can I help you?" he asked, sitting beside her on the pew. "I do not believe we have been introduced, have we?"

Sarah didn't look up, but shook her head in response.

"I am Father Patrick. How may I help you today?"

"You can't," Sarah replied bluntly. "There's nothing to be done anymore. I just wish there was some way we could get away from Janet Baxter. I came here before and was given a crucifix and water."

"My child, there is nothing in this world beyond help. Everyone can be helped. It isn't too late. Ever." Father Patrick wasn't sure exactly how he intended to help her, but he knew what he had to say.

"We can go back, you mean? Get the crucifix, the water and leave? Janet Baxter said--"

At once, the priest's tone changed. "You've spoken to her? My child, you need to get away from that house, and never return. Based on what has happened there before, child, if you have communicated with the evil … the day you return to the house is the day you will lose the option of leaving."

"Do you mean they will kill us if we go back?" Sarah asked. Although she thought she knew the answer, she needed confirmation.

The priest stared intently at his feet, doing his utmost to avoid making eye contact.

"Tell me the truth. No lies, no evasion. No omissions. I need to know."

Father Patrick's lips moved, apparently in prayer, yet no words came out. Sarah, growing more irate by the second, wanted nothing more than to demand an answer. However, interrupting a prayer seemed wrong. She couldn't do that. Instead, she sat, waiting for him to finish.

Finally, Father Patrick spoke. "Yes, my child. Evil has you marked. The day you go back is the day you will die."

"Well, we're staying in the hotel at the moment. We are very likely to leave the house and the town. But we need to get our things before we do."

He shook his head vehemently and grabbed her by the hand. "My child, you must not go back to that house. Ever. Not even for your things. You can buy new things. This world … your things … all of it is temporary."

"Well, why did Bradley Taylor sell us the house? If you all knew these things, why?"

Father Patrick shook his head in disgust. "Bradley Taylor is a man obsessed with his career. He did not think anything would happen, and didn't believe until after the house was sold."

"What should we do then? Our car is parked there, and we have no other means of transportation."

"All you can do now is leave the house, maybe even the town, and pray for protection." Father Patrick spoke gently, but firmly. It was an instruction as opposed to advice.

"Let me stop you right there," Sarah snapped, not appreciating his tone. "I'm not the praying type."

"Whether you are the praying type or not, my child, isn't it worth a try?" he said, his tone pleading. He looked at Sarah with wide, tear-filled eyes. Sarah shook her head, and told him she wasn't going to pray, that she was an atheist.

"May evil flee from your door, child," the priest concluded, and stood up to walk away. "I'm sorry but, unless you are staying for Mass, you need to leave now."

Without another word, Sarah jumped to her feet and made her way out of the cathedral. As she left, people started flocking in, bumping into her as they entered.

***

Franklin had decided against going into the library and had instead headed into an odd little shop on the corner of the high street. He was immediately hit with an intoxicating, earthy stench. A ludicrous number of bizarre plants littered the floor, and crystals were strung up around the room, which was lit by green lanterns.

Above his head, wind chimes sounded, and brought his presence to the attention of a woman standing in a corner. There were countless beads in her hair, which clinked together with every movement of her head. She wore a green woven headband, and her eyes were wild.

"Welcome to my shop," she sang, her voice shrill and piercing. "What would you like to buy from me? What would you like to buy from precious Adeola?"

Franklin answered, "I'm not certain what I need – be it plants or crystals, I don't know."

"What do you need them for?" Adeola asked, swaying around the room like the wind, her beads clattering and clinking. Her wild eyes burrowed into his.

"Repelling evil spirits," Franklin said.

This stopped the woman in her tracks. She stared at him with those wild eyes and bared her teeth. Unperturbed, Franklin repeated himself and then asked, "Do you have anything for that?"

Adeola tilted back her head, opened her mouth, and an ungodly cackle burst out of it. Sounding more and more insane with every noise she made, the woman said, "Of course I do. Precious Adeola has remedies for every situation, every emotion."

Widening his eyes, he asked, "What do I need?"

The woman smiled an unsettling, toothy grin, and yanked two crystals out of a drawer. "This," she sang, "is labradorite, and this is black tourmaline. Take them." She handed him the crystals and returned to the corner in which she had been standing when he entered the shop. She lifted an amethyst out of a box, and tiptoed back over to Franklin, as though frightened of dropping it.

"Is it radioactive?" Franklin joked. It was a freedom he hadn't realised before. People don't understand the value of smiling despite the awful circumstances that life throws at you.

Adeola looked at him, eyebrows raised in confusion. Upon realising he was vainly attempting to be funny, she cackled with pity. "No, it is not."

Handing the crystal over, she told him the price, but before she had even finished the sentence she stopped. "Wait," she suddenly whispered. "Are you him?"

"Who do you think I am?" Franklin asked, confused.

"Are you the man who just moved into the house at the top of the hill?" she asked, her eyes widening, and glistening in the light. When Franklin didn't immediately answer, her eyes widened in anger, and she snapped, "I said…"

"Yes," Franklin answered, "I am. I moved in there with my wife."

"Why?" Adeola demanded, shaking her head in frustration. "Don't you know what goes on there? You have to get out of there. You have to leave. You don't understand."

Franklin stared at her, and informed her that he hadn't been told until after they had moved in, that he had taken his wife there for a new start, to begin a new life. "I wish more than anything now that we had gone for the other house, the one in Scotland."

"Take the crystals. No charge," Adeola said, her voice deepening as though she were trying not to cry. Franklin thanked her, but she said quickly, "Of course, if you die, I'll be taking them back."

Franklin snorted, abruptly amused at the remark. "Thanks for the encouragement," he said.

Adeola didn't return the smile. "That is free of charge, also," she replied. "Please be careful. Life isn't a chip with which you gamble. Leave the house: be safe. Stay in the house: tempt death. That woman is cruel and unforgiving. She will not stop until you are dead. Unless you leave that place, you will not survive. May the crystals be your refuge."

She stalked away into the shadows, until she could no longer be seen. Franklin turned and walked out of the shop, into the sunlight.

***

It was almost midday by the time Franklin and Sarah met again. They decided to return to the hotel.

As they walked, Sarah explained what had happened in the cathedral. Franklin, irritated by the priest's flippant brush-off of their fears, said, "And that's why I didn't come to the church with you. I don't have time for people who see everything like that. Life is hard. We can't wave a magic wand and have a few thousand pounds to buy ourselves new things."

"I know – that's why I didn't suggest it," Sarah retorted.

Shaking his head vehemently, Franklin went on to tell his wife about his experience with the woman in the shop on the corner. "That's when I bumped into you," he finished.

"Anything's worth a try at this point," Sarah whispered, turning to look around at the people who were trying, but failing, to hide the fact that they were staring at them.

Grabbing a gawking passer-by, Sarah demanded, "Why are people avoiding us?" Although she knew the answer, she wanted an explanation.

Dumbstruck, the man spun around, as though looking for a way to avoid the conversation. There was nothing he could do but tell the truth. "It's nothing to do with our opinion of you," he said, his voice almost a whisper. It was almost as if he was trying to hide the fact, he was explaining things to Franklin and Sarah, which did nothing to ease her rising frustration. "We know the mark, you see."

"No," Sarah replied. "I don't. Explain."

"You've been marked by that place, by that woman. You have the black aura."

"What do you mean?" Franklin asked, trying to keep his emotions reigned in. "Marked for what?"

"Death," the man said. "There's nothing you can do to get out of it. I'm sorry."

Sarah turned to look at Franklin, unsure what to say or do. Everything – all the hope, all the longing to fight – had been pulled out of her. "In that case, we're fighting a losing battle."

"I'm sorry," the man said again. "Truly I am." His eyes fell to the ground. Slowly, he turned to move away. Neither Franklin nor Sarah cared any more what he did. They just wanted peace and to be left alone to live their lives.

Although they no longer cared about the people avoiding them, they were infuriated by the fact that nobody had been willing to tell them anything, or to help.

Fury built up inside Franklin, and he utilised every ounce of resistance in his body to keep from allowing the fire within his blood, within his very being, to pour out, engulfing anything and anyone in its path.

"We've paid for the night at the hotel," he said, the venom in his voice audible to Sarah despite its softness. "We're going to stay there tonight, and go back tomorrow. I am not giving up that easily."

Sarah put her open hand next to Franklin's, and Franklin took it, and grasped it tightly in his own. "Neither am I," Sarah said. "Whatever happens, whatever this life throws at us, it's meaningless. All that matters is that we are together. So long as we are together, we can face anything. With you by my side, with me by yours, we'll take on the world."

Franklin couldn't help but smile. Those words came directly from Sarah's wedding vows to him. Two years before, they had been so happy and carefree. Nothing could have prepared them for what the subsequent years would bring, the anguish and agony that was coming for them.

"Do you remember," Franklin began, "the day we met?"

"Of course I do. We bumped into each other in the cafeteria, and you immediately started to smile at me when you saw I was crying. It was the only smile I had seen all day. My grandfather had just died, and your first words to me were—"

"Whatever has happened, you are strong enough to get through it," Franklin recalled.

"I knew there and then that we were going to be friends."

"Things were so simple back then. We were free."

"We can be again. We will not be broken or destroyed by this. I promise you, Frank, we are going to get through this. One way or another. We are going to come through this together. Whatever happens."

Hand in hand, they returned to the hotel room. Above the town, the clouds darkened, enveloping everyone and everything in shadow.

As the minutes stretched into hours, Franklin and Sarah sat on the hotel bed, hands entwined, reminiscing about times long gone and memories they cherished. For those few hours, in spite of everything going on in their lives, they laughed. The power of memories lies in the fact that they can be so many things: a comfort, a blessing, a burden, a trauma.

As day became night, the town was cloaked in darkness. Lingering in the dark, loitering outside the hotel room, waiting for the couple to fall asleep were the Baxters. Janet knew what she was going to do, and she knew how she would draw them back to the house so she could carry out what she had promised.

They believed they could fool me, Janet thought, amusement bubbling through her. They tried to tell me they are good people. For that, they will pay dearly.

Inside the hotel room, Franklin and Sarah kissed and, leaving the light on, started to drift slowly into dreams. Every so often, they would awake with a start, thrusting themselves into a sitting position, their eyes darting here and there.

As the night dragged on, though, they finally fell asleep. With a smile, Janet Baxter began her work.

Chapter Eleven

Janet Baxter moved with deathly elegance as she set her plan into action. Watching those pathetic people sleep, a smirk spread across her face. They believed they were safe, she thought, her smile widening. Fools. You are never safe from death.

Baxter's flame-orange glow touched every section of the grotesque little hotel room. Her gaze darted from the cretin of a man to the pathetic woman. Grinning, she glided across the room and hovered above Sarah's unconscious body.

Terrified by her dream, Sarah tossed and turned, her body writhing in fear. An idea came into Janet Baxter's head. Snapping her fingers, she woke up the sad excuse for a man lying next to the thrashing woman.

Slowly, Franklin's eyes adjusted to the ominous spectral glare. At last, he saw the mother hovering above his wife.

He opened his mouth to scream for help, and went to try and shield his darling wife with his own body. With another snap of her fingers, Janet Baxter held him in place. Alas, there was nothing Franklin could do to stop the demon.

As Franklin stared, Janet Baxter's colour shifted from orange to a deathly red, and then an unearthly mist obscured her from view. In the fog, that vicious colour filled Sarah's eyes, and she let out a breath … her final breath. Franklin cried her name and did everything he could to try and get out of the beast's control. He screamed and screamed. But nobody would hear him.

He begged for a higher being to help him. But no protection was coming. All his efforts were in vain. Sarah, his darling wife, was gone, lost between life and death. Although her spirit fought for control, her body was the plaything of Janet Baxter.

If only the poor man had known what was about to happen, he would have wished for his wonderful other half to be dead. Dead people cannot be used. The dead cannot hurt or be hurt. Alas, he was unaware. And so, alone in that room, he sat sobbing uncontrollably beside the shell of the woman he had married.

Surrounded by red mist, he could do nothing but cry.

He lost all track of time until the fog vanished, and the body of Sarah shook into consciousness. It was not her own consciousness, however. Sarah was now the tool of Janet Baxter.

When Sarah's eyes opened, they were as red as the fires of hell. Franklin scrambled away.

Once again, Sarah thrashed and writhed on the bed. As her spirit relinquished control, with contorted movements, Sarah's body clambered to its feet.

Despite Franklin's valiant efforts to move after his wife as she glided across the hotel room, he could do nothing. Although he knew the woman he loved was gone, he couldn't believe it. He loved her so much. If only love could bring someone back – but then where would we be?

Watching his wife glide out of the room, and out of his sight, Franklin prayed for his death to be swift. This is all my fault, he thought, tears streaming down his cheeks. I wanted to come here; Sarah had wanted the house up north.

Unable, unwilling, to move, he sat in the hotel room, alone with his self-loathing, his only companion. Darkness cloaked the town and his broken heart. An invisible force kept him on that cold, hard floor, weighing down on him like a wet blanket.

At that same moment, his wife left the hotel, heading back to the house.

Finally, the hellish force released its grip on Franklin as though it had never been there. In one swift movement, Franklin was on his feet. Hastily, he moved through the hotel. He understood he had to go straight to that house. That accursed house.

Above his head, the sky was black. No moonlight lit his path. At the foot of the hill that led to the house, he was hit with guilt: he should have protected Sarah as he had promised. He had failed her. She had relied on him, trusted him to take care of her. And he had failed.

Franklin started up the hill, not caring about his own safety, not knowing or worrying about what was coming. Though he tried, he couldn't remember happier times. Truth be told, he couldn't recall what happiness felt like. It was as if every good and pleasant memory, every good and pleasant fibre of his being, had been drained out of him.

Bitter cold sunk its teeth into his flesh, and terror shrouded around his body. An eerie silence prevailed. Even the sounds of the night had deadened. All he could hear was shallow breathing.

And then he was outside the house.

The house towered over him, but this did nothing but galvanise Franklin's bravery. Before he knew it, his hand was on the door handle.

Locked, of course.

With one swift, forceful kick, the door flew open and crashed into the table behind it.

All Franklin's fear was gone, lost forever. All he wanted was to get Sarah to safety. He didn't care if he survived or not, so long as she was safe. He would not be afraid. He would not be defeated.

He screamed Sarah's name, the exploding out of him. This godforsaken place, cloaked in darkness, inhabited by hatred itself ... this was supposed to be their new start. Instead, it had been their downfall.

Within the depths of that place devoid of mercy, Janet Baxter smiled. Watching as the pathetic street urchin searched every room for his ridiculous woman, her grin grew. She's not coming back, Janet Baxter thought, a triumphant grin curving the corners of her mouth. Your little wife is gone. Soon, you will be too. Goodbye, Oswalds.

Sarah's voice carried through the Baxter dominion, sweet, innocent, gentle. It called Franklin's name, the voice moving from place to place … but it was not her speaking.

When Franklin heard her, false hope sprung up from within him. Before he even knew where it was coming from, he was running up the stairs, ready to get Sarah and get out of this hell.

Her voice sounded again. Again. Again. Each time, it sounded further away. "I'm in the bedroom, please come and help me. Please hurry."

Stumbling over his own feet, Franklin crashed down the corridor, guided only by his determination. A gentle orange glow flickered from inside the bedroom. As he neared the door, the glow flickered wildly.

Franklin began to dash into the bedroom just as the door slammed. Screams sounded from beyond the door. Franklin cried Sarah's name again and again. Desperation replaced determination within seconds.

"Get back from the door!" he yelled, grabbing a chair from the opposite room. Launching the chair through the air, he splintered the door, sending wooden shrapnel to the floor. He ran into the bedroom.

Relief overwhelmed him. There, standing in front of him, holding a lantern above her head, was Sarah.

"Goodbye, my love," her voice said.

Before Franklin realised what was happening, Sarah Marie Oswald – the woman he had loved since he had met her, the woman he had sworn to protect – threw the lantern to the ground. Shattering, it spread flames through the room, surrounding her instantly.

Fire engulfed the room, spreading quicker than Franklin could think, quicker than he could even move. All around him, the flames grew, threatening to consume him as they had his wife.

Franklin saw Sarah sway across the room. He ran to grab her and get her out of there. Janet Baxter moved Sarah before Franklin could slow down. He smashed through the window and started falling to the ground below.

Falling. Falling. Falling.

He was moments away from death, but all he could do was fall.

He wasn't worried or scared or anxious. He was relieved and excited. He was going to a place that has no pain, no suffering and no more death. He couldn't be hurt anymore.

With a thump, he hit the ground and breathed his last.

***

All night, the blaze roared, the almighty volume awakening the entire town. Nobody moved until that place, forsaken by happiness and love, came crashing to the ground. In a frenzy, the population ran to the house to help in any way they could. But they were too late.

Below the bedroom window, Franklin was sprawled out on the ground, his face distorted by the impact of the fall. Sarah ... well, she was never found. When the remains of the house had been cleared, her body was gone.

A question asked by a young child lingered in the dark: "If the house is destroyed, is the evil gone?"

Father Patrick answered bluntly, "Alas, dear child, this house contained the evil for decades. Either due to the flames, or the demolition, the evil has been released into the world and I fear we are in more danger than ever before."

He was right.

Andrew Lamont
THE END

ACKNOWLEDGEMENTS

First and foremost, I would like to thank my readers. To everyone who has followed me online, to everyone who has sent support, to everyone who picked up Miscellany, or Are You Well? thank you! It is thanks to your generosity that I can continue to write books, something I dreamed of doing since I was five. Now, it is reality. Thank you.

Thank you, thank you, thank you, Ross Cockrill. Thank you for being my best friend, and for helping me through so much this year. Thank you for always encouraging me when I wanted to give up. Without your help and support, this book would not exist. Thank you for the laughs, the memories, the coffees, the steel beam distractions. For everything. Never change.

To my wonderful cousin, Anna Knecht, thank you for the constant love and support you give me. Thank you so much for always being there for me. I love you.

Thanks are also due to both Naomi Farrimond and Chloe Martin for being excited about the initial idea of this book even before I was, for believing in it before I did. Without them, I'd never have written this. Thank you both!

As always, thank you so much to Martin Clarke, Scott MacDonald, and the Hillview Young Adults for supporting me all these years, for calling me out when I need it, and for making me a better person. I don't think I could ever express how much I appreciate you all.

Thank you to the people who constantly remind me that, in spite of what I write, there is good in the world. The greatest friends anyone could have: Trendon Hazel, Abi Salseg, Mason Stone, Lathan Nichols, Josh Young, Jaden Young, Masi Bruning.

Where would I be without Jenna Moreci? For supporting me, always calming me down when I'm stressing and being a wonderful person, thank you!

Thank you to Leigh Bardugo for making it clear to me that I should write what I want to write, for constantly inspiring and motivating me, and so many others.

To Jane Kelsey, Trina Rowland, Demi Conard, Olivia Bennett, Mel Ingrid, Stella Day and Karis Tomic, thank you for everything.

Of course, thank you to all the teachers who believed in and supported me through my school years and beyond. Teachers really do make people.

Finally, thank you to the authors who make this community so fantastic, and for welcoming me so openly: Lindsay Cummings, Kim Chance, Alwyn Hamilton, Gareth L Powell, Sara Holland, V.E. Schwab, Victoria Aveyard, Susan Dennard, Natalie Banks,

Danielle Paige, Angie Thomas, and so many more.

www.ingramcontent.com/pod-product-compliance
Lightning Source LLC
Chambersburg PA
CBHW021149130626
46554CB00005B/1736